Beyond Someday

BY *JIM SAGE*

Dorrance Publishing Co
585 Alpha Drive
Pittsburgh, PA 15238
Visit our website at *www.dorrancebookstore.com*

ISBN: 978-1-6366-1469-4
eISBN: 978-1-6366-1727-5

Beyond Someday

Dedication

This book is dedicated to my late, loving wife, Carolyn Ruth Sage. During all our years together, she somehow found the courage to forgive my many, many faults, overlook the many mistakes I made, and always tried to bring out the best in me - I know that was no easy task. I can say, without reservation, my life has been a wonderful journey, but only because she was there for the largest part of it. I cannot imagine my life without her.

Chapter I

Carolyn carefully placed her favorite linen marker between the pages, closed the book, and gently laid it on the table in front of her.

"Another love story almost finished," she said aloud as if talking to a silent partner somewhere in the room.

As she removed her reading glasses and placed them on top of the book, she thought, *Reading seems to take much more time these days. I suppose that's just one more part of getting older.*

She slowly rose to her feet, walked to a large picture window overlooking Lake Mill Pond, and gazed out at the cold, winter landscape. A light rain was falling and seemed to dance across the water to the tune of a melody only Mother Nature could hear. A breeze moved the bare branches of her favorite birch tree in rhythm to the music as they danced with the rain. Low-hanging clouds cast a dismal, gray color across the sky making her feel as if she was part of a cold scene captured on some artist's dismal canvas. *You might think Mother Nature would be a bit more accommodating on a girl's ninetieth birthday*, she thought.

"Perhaps just a little sunshine could have made this big day a bit more cheerful," she said under her breath.

She pulled her sweater tighter across her chest as a chill moved up and down her slender back, then shifted her weight to her good, right leg. Her left leg had not been the same since she fell trying to get out of a tight booth at her favorite restaurant a couple years ago.

"If Jim had been here, he would have held me tight and prevented the fall. The doctors must have missed something because on days like today it hurts like hell," she mused.

Her gaze focused on the dismal, winter landscape for the longest time as she shifted her weight from right to left and back again every few minutes as if trying to dance to the silent music playing outside her window. She moved her right hand to her chest and rubbed gently to ease that nagging little pain deep inside.*Yeah, yeah*, she thought. *I know I shouldn't make that chili anymore, heartburn is too painful, but I still dearly love the flavor.*

As the pain subsided, she folded her hands together across her slender waist, watching Mother Nature's carefully orchestrated dance recital unfold in front of her across the lake. This was the view she had planned with her late husband Jim as they designed and built their retirement home. Each step in the process had been taken with careful attention to every detail. Carolyn saw to that. Her ability to focus on every detail had been a lifesaver more than once. Both knew once construction was complete, they would have to live with their mistakes. But if mistakes were there, neither Carolyn nor Jim could see them because both loved the house as if it had a life of its own.

Jim often said, "This house has more personality and character than a lot of people I know." This was the place they had chosen together; this was the place they both loved more than anywhere else on the planet. This is where home would be as they passed their retirement years together!

Her mind drifted back to their first night in the new home, a bottle of German wine, the radio playing softly as they began to unpack.

She briskly shook her head to clear her mind saying, "No, no, I'm much too old to be thinking about that kind of stuff."

Carolyn's health had always been good. Even as she passed into what everyone referred to as the golden years, she did not suffer what Jim would call "old-fart aches and pains". A tinge of arthritis in the fingers perhaps, but for the most part, when everyone else was down and out, Carolyn was at the top of her game; she was the caregiver. Her mind was amazingly clear, no signs of forgetfulness, no difficulty recalling details of events occurring long, long ago. Her doctors continued to be surprised by the consistent excellence of her overall physical and mental condition. Recently she had complained of mild heartburn, but she knew that was only caused by eating certain foods she loved, ones that no longer agreed with her.

"Hmm," she would say, "my doctors might not be able to tell that I'm getting older, but my stomach sure knows it." She always liked to tell her friends, "I can remember sixteen years old like it was yesterday."

She gazed at the reflection of herself projected back from the glass window. All the curves were still in the right places, her 5'10" height seemed to force all the visible body parts into their proper place in the right proportions. She had been slender and shapely all her life and still had a good figure. Her short hair had turned from auburn brown to silver gray to white, but she had it cut and styled every month or so and it looked no worse for years of wear and tear. Her figure was still slender as it had been all her life - pregnancies excluded, of course - but the wrinkles in her face finally had their way and the once smooth skin was proof positive that she was not thirty-nine anymore! Other than that, she was strikingly beautiful for her age, the good looks and good figure did a nice job of hiding ninety years that had gone before. *Hmm, not bad for an old broad*, she thought.

She placed her hands on her hips, pushed them forward and then posed, for a moment, as a New York model might, but quickly found that position to be a bit uncomfortable. *Too old for that stuff*, she thought as she folded her arms across her chest tightly to hold the sweater in place against the cold and continued her stare across Lake Mill Pond at the cold, silent winter scene.

Carolyn's solitude was broken by the sound of a door opening, behind her. She turned quickly to see her granddaughter Fallon come in with her children Samantha and Michael in tow.

"Nice move, MaMaw," said Fallon. "Put that step to music and you will be a very rich lady."

"Thank you Punkin! My babies," cried Carolyn as she held out her arms to the great-grandchildren.

Both children ran to their great-grandmother and threw their arms around her lovingly.

"I had not expected you this early," said Carolyn as she hugged each child tightly.

Samantha smiled and stretched to kiss her great-grandmother on the cheek.

"I'm sorry, the weather is so bad. I suppose we will have to roast marshmallows in the fireplace because we can't take the boat out today" said Carolyn with a look of apology on her face.

"That's okay Mom," said her daughter, Robin, as she limped through the doorway.The brass tip on her cane made a hollow sound as it tapped the hardwood floor with each step she took. Robin had struggled with arthritis in her knees most of her life. The constant pain made walking a real adventure. But she was not one to complain and always tried to make the best of a bad situation. In her youth, Robin had a petite figure, never weighing more than 110 pounds with long brown hair framing a tiny, oval face. Carolyn often described her appearance as the family Kewpie doll.

Robin recently retired after a successful career as an accounting manager. After graduation from Old Dominion University, she finished her master's at Clemson University and enjoyed a career as a nationally recognized authority on control of post-contract cost escalation in the commercial construction industry. She taught at her beloved Clemson University for many years until arthritis in her knees and hips made a simple chore like standing in front of a class or walking to the bathroom an extremely difficult undertaking. Now she spent all her time in her

beach-front home overlooking the ocean at Virginia Beach.

"How was the drive?" Carolyn asked.

"Not bad," Fallon replied. "We seem to have missed most of the traffic. Perhaps everyone is staying inside on a cold day like today."

"We watched *Jack and the Beanstalk* on the car TV, MaMaw," announced Mike.

"One of my favorites," Carolyn replied as she patted Mike on his curly head.

"I would rather watch *Sleeping Beauty*," Samantha injected, "But it was his turn to choose."

"Oh, if only your PaPaw Jim could see the two of you now. He would be so proud," said Carolyn as tears welled up in her eyes.

"That's okay, MaMaw," whispered Samantha. "We talk to him every night."

Carolyn brushed away the tears with the sleeve of her sweater just as a tall, strikingly handsome man walked through the door. He stopped, smiled at everyone, waved his big arms in front of himself, and said, "Did someone say there was a birthday party going on here?"

Edward Michael Carter, Fallon's husband, was a good-looking man. His 6'2" height, accompanied by a well chiseled 220 pounds, dwarfed everyone around him. His naturally blonde hair and emerald green eyes punctuated his striking, memorable appearance. When Fallon stood next to him with her 5'11" height, slender figure, and long, shoulder length brown hair, they made a truly striking couple, appearing more as a television commercial might. Fallon and Edward met in college, went through graduate school together, and now they were going through life together.

"Just like me and PaPaw," Carolyn said to herself. "They are a matched set."

"Did you say something, Mom?" Robin asked

"No dear, just thinking what a beautiful family you all make together," replied Carolyn with a big smile.

Edward took two big strides across the room and wrapped his big arms around Carolyn.

"Happy birthday, pretty lady," he said as he kissed her on the cheek.

"With the exceptions of Robin, Fallon, and Sam, you are still the prettiest girl I know," he whispered.

Carolyn blushed and patted Edward on his broad chest.

"My granddaughter is a lucky lady," she said with a big smile on her face.

Fallon stood-up from her chair and announced, "Okay, everyone in the kitchen. Time to get ready for a party."

As if rehearsed, everyone started moving toward the kitchen at the same time. Fallon slowly backed away, holding the door, as everyone passed through into the kitchen. She immediately took charge of the crowd and started giving instructions to each individual. Everyone began working their individual tasks with the precision of a marching band. Before very long, the coffee pot was cooking, the cake was out of its box and sitting on the dining room table, glasses and silverware were placed for each setting, soft drinks were opened and ready to pour, and the lighting on the chandelier was turned down to soften the ever-changing scene.*Very good*, thought Fallon as she watched everyone go about their work.

Fallon had turned out to be a take-charge lady. Her training at graduate school and the PhD program at University of Virginia had taught the benefits of aggressive, methodical leadership as she worked through the rigid and difficult Bio-Chemistry program. After graduation, she worked as a researcher at Bio-Matrix Laboratories and soon began to make herself known for innovation and thinking "outside the box". It took her only four years to discover a link between a breakdown in the enzyme chain controlling functionality of mitochondria DNA in female breast tissue and the onset of breast cancer. Her discoveries soon allowed her to reverse the enzyme breakdown resulting in not only a cure for the disease, but development of a chemical process allowing the immune system to distinguish between cancer cells and those that are normal. That allowed the immune system to attack and destroy the bad cells, while preserving the good ones. Several medical authorities said history will most

likely label her as the one who discovered the first true cure for a form of cancer, setting the medical stage for application of her solution to all other forms of the disease. Her colleagues applauded the many awards she received for her research and discoveries. Now, only a few years later, she was head of the research department at Bio-Matrix, managing the efforts of over 250 scientists and researchers.

As Fallon watched the kitchen workers go about their chores, chimes of the front door sounded the arrival of more family members to attend the party.

"I'll get it," she announced to everyone.

She opened the door and there standing in front of her were Uncle Allen, Aunt Joan, and Aunt Lori.

"Come in, come in!" she enthusiastically invited. "I am so happy to see you. Your arrival is right on time. MaMaw will be so happy to see you."

Allen and Joan both wrapped their arms around Fallon and hugged her for the longest time.

"Okay, Okay, enough," commanded Lori. "My turn."

Lori embraced Fallon and kissed her on the cheek.

"I have missed you so much, sweetheart," Lori whispered.

Allen closed the heavy front door with a shove and took the girls' coats as he moved toward the closet. He saw Edward as he passed the kitchen door and shouted, "I suppose you know where a fellow can get a drink around here?"

Edward looked up from the punch bowl he was filling and winked.

"Sure," he laughed, "I know where they hide the good stuff. Oh, by the way, MaMaw saved some of her most recent chili just for you. She says she can't eat it anymore."Allen and Joan had been incredibly successful in their careers as bankers. Both had completed their master's programs and rose to the position of president of their banks while enjoying all the financial benefits banking executives might expect. Now, both had just turned seventy, retired from the everyday working world, and were living in an upscale community just outside Jacksonville, Florida overlooking a very large lake surrounded by a private golf course with an exclusive country club.

Allen was Jim's son from his first marriage. A tour in the navy after high school had taught him the importance of success in everything he did. Immediately after discharge from the navy, Allen attended the University of Washington, majoring in business administration with a minor in finance. After finishing the baccalaureate degree and a master's in business finance, he had embarked on a career in the banking industry. From the very start, he was destined to become successful. But he was no match for Joan. She was a straight "A" student through graduate school, clearly destined to eventually land at the top. Allen often said that Joan was one of the few people he met in his life that had "senior executive" written all over her. Together they achieved enviable reputations not only in the domestic banking industry, but in the international banking family as well.

Allen's 5'8" height was well formed by weight lifting and physical training of his youth. His curly, reddish-brown hair and blue eyes gave him the appearance of a mischievous little boy. Joan's figure looked more like that of a model than a mother of two children. All the curves were in the right places, giving her 5'7" height a youthful appearance. She wore her salt and pepper hair short-cropped around her oval face. Their two daughters, Abigail and Olivia, had both completed graduate school. Allen and Joan would not settle for anything less than that.

Abigail landed a very lucrative position as an international account executive for an American oil corporation while Olivia was finishing her PhD in economics. Unfortunately, both girls were on overseas assignments that would take them well through the Christmas and New Year holidays. Olivia was working on a grant from the United Nations to develop an economic model to be used as part of a multi-national recovery program for underdeveloped countries on the African continent. Abigail was leading an American negotiating team organized by the federal government trying to reach an international agreement on stabilization of international petroleum prices. Clearly, Allen and Joan had much to be proud of.

Edward met Allen at the kitchen door with his favorite drink, Jack Daniels and ginger ale. Both were glad to see each other. They had much in common. Edward was a graduate of University of Virginia medical school and had gone on to become an internationally known thoracic surgeon. Edward's development of new surgical procedures, especially for cardiac surgery, made his name a household word in medical circles around the globe. At the same time, Allen's work in the international banking community had made him a hero to small businesses struggling every day for survival. Lori had devoted her life to the protection and defense of animals. After graduation from University of Virginia veterinarian school, Lori went on to become a staunch advocate of animal rights. Her work in rescue and adoption of abandoned animals became a national standard. Surprisingly enough, the financial rewards for her work had been considerable. Now retired, she devoted her time to writing from her New Hampshire home perched at the top of a very high mountain. Her husband, Paul, had died several years earlier when the brakes of his car failed causing it to plunge over a cliff to a rocky canyon, 900 feet below. From that point, Lori decided to devote herself to her work.

Finally, the last guest arrived. Beverly Ransome had been Carolyn's lifelong friend. They met just after Carolyn's marriage to her first husband and became life-long friends. Bev had a long career with the government as a resource security officer at the bureau of printing and engraving. Her final assignment with the bureau was in the Dallas, Texas office where she retired on her sixty-fifth birthday. Bev bought an ocean-side condo in Virginia Beach, Virginia - just forty-five minutes from Carolyn in Williamsburg and a short walk to Robin's home – where she lived comfortably, often visiting her old friend Carolyn. "Sorry I'm late," she announced as Fallon escorted her through the door and into the foyer.

"Damn traffic between here and the beach is impossible. So, what are we drinking besides Geritol?" she joked.

Beverly had been a beauty in her youth. Her 5'3" height, petite figure, with long blonde hair and deep blue eyes caught the attention of everyone around her.

"Lite beer coming up," Allen called out as Bev walked into the kitchen.

With all the guests in attendance, the party started. The remainder of the day and most of the evening was devoted to the birthday party. Everyone ate far too much, drank more than enough German wine, and sang happy birthday so many times no one ever wanted to hear that song again. Everyone had a wonderful time, but, alas, as the hour grew late, the younger ones finally came to the end of their rope and were more than ready for bed.

"Time to play with the angels," MaMaw announced.

PaPaw had told Fallon when she was two years old that children didn't really go to sleep at night. They went to bed, closed their eyes, then go to play with the angels. Through the years, that thought had stuck and now bedtime was playtime with the angels.

Mike and Sam both ran to their great-grandmother, grabbing her hand tightly.

"Tell us a bed time story MaMaw, please," Mike pleaded with anticipation.

Carolyn smiled at her babies. How could she not agree?

"A bed time story it is," agreed MaMaw as she took their little hands and started up the stairs.

Once the teeth had been brushed, street clothes exchanged for pajamas, and both children were tucked into their beds, Carolyn settled into the comfortable chair between the beds.

"Which story would you like to hear?" she asked.

"I want to hear about the beautiful princess and her handsome prince," Samantha announced.

Carolyn settled back in the chair, rolled her eyes and thought, *Oh me, I have told this story so many times, how do I come up with one more unique version? There are only so many versions of Cinderella and the handsome prince!*

Carolyn's mind raced, then the light of discovery came on as she settled in her chair with a big smile on her face.

"Okay, but since both of you are getting a little older, perhaps it is time for a story that is closer to real? How about a story about two people who are very close to you and you know very well?" she asked.

"MaMaw, that sounds exciting," Mike exclaimed, "Tell us the story."

Carolyn looked up at the ceiling as she settled herself in the chair.

"Pay attention PaPaw, you are about to become a fairy tale," she said softly to herself so the children could not hear.

Carolyn placed her hand in her lap, took another deep breath, and began the story.

"Once upon a time, in a land not so far away, at a time not so long ago, there lived a beautiful Princess name Carolyn and her handsome Prince named Jim…"Now, the story begins…

Chapter II

Carolyn Wilder sat in the living room of her parent's Fairfax, Virginia home, lost in thought as she tried to figure out how to get into a good college knowing her family could not pay for it. Mom and Dad were at work, sisters Peggy and Sharon had gone shopping together, brother Billy was outside in the front yard playing with his friends while Kirk, the youngest brother, was asleep in his room. It was Carolyn's turn to keep her eye on the two younger brothers for a day.*I know I should be preparing to attend college, but I just don't see how that is possible*, she thought as she stared out the living room window watching her brother play in the front yard.

Summer break from high school was almost over and had passed uneventfully. She had started dating a nice boy, George Hecht, the brother of her sister Peggy's boyfriend, Jimmy. George was the youngest and a bit more settled down than Jimmy. He was the quiet, shy type and did not like to dance very much, but then again most of the boys she knew failed in that department. George had a lot of qualities Carolyn liked! He was kind, gentle, and generous to a fault. The fact that he was tall with dish-water blond hair and blue eyes also helped a lot.

Carolyn's mother, Geraldine, and father, Cot, both worked full time jobs to support a big family. Peggy was a senior in high school, Sharon was getting ready to start the sixth grade, brother Bill was in grade school, and Kirk was not yet ready for kindergarten.

"How in the world will Mom and Dad be able to continue supporting the family and send me to college at the same time?" she wondered. *Perhaps I will get a scholarship*, she thought. *No, not me, I have good grades, but I am not a straight 'A' student and that's what it takes to get a scholarship.* She wrinkled her nose at the thought and made a sour face as her mood worsened. *I'll be 17 soon! Perhaps I can get a part-time job and start saving money for tuition. George Mason University is here in Fairfax, so I could live at home. That would certainly hold down expenses!* Her mood improved as she started working out the details in her head.

"Yes, yes, yes!" she exclaimed. "When Mom comes home from work today I'll ask her if the government would hire a high school student to work part-time. I bet that would work!" she said to herself, proud that she had been able to solve the problem all by herself.

Little did she know, later in life, her ability to reduce complex problems to their simplest terms then logically attack the problem would result in an uncanny ability to quickly come up with practical solutions. This skill would become one of her greatest assets as she pursued a career in which dealing with and solving complex problems would be an every-day chore.

Carolyn's mood had now gone full circle. She was her usual happy, cheerful self. Thoughts of going to school, working a part-time job, and getting ready for college all at the same time had made her day. She made a mental note to discuss her solution with Peggy.

Her sister had confided in her that she intended to marry Jimmy soon as they were both out of high school. Both Jimmy and Peggy were entering their senior year in high school, so that big event would not wait much longer. Peggy was not interested in going to college. She thought a good job in a department store or the admin office of a local business might help her and Jimmy start their life together while he established himself in a good job with a bright career path for the future.

Carolyn stood up, checked on her brother in the front yard, looked in on Kirk, then walked back to her bedroom to change her sweater.

"George will be coming by soon and I don't want him to see me in this old, worn and tattered sweatshirt," she told herself.

She removed the shirt and stood in front of the full-length mirror at the end of her bed.

"Hmm, not too bad for a sixteen-year-old," she observed *Perhaps a bit tall, bet I reach 5'10" or so before it's all over. My chest has gotten bigger and I am not fat. I hope the boys like tall, slender girls*, she thought hopefully. Her shoulder-length brown hair framed her face as if to highlight her light complexion. She was tall and slender now, but the roots of natural beauty to come later were clearly evident.

She pulled on a light sweater; posed for a moment and said to herself, *That will have to do.*

There were no answers of reassurance, just faint noises of kids playing outside. She smiled to herself and walked back into the living room to wait for George.

The summer of 1959 passed quickly and uneventfully. Peggy and Jimmy finally announced their engagement with plans to marry in the fall. Carolyn continued to date George when he was not too busy with his friends doing whatever boys do when they are together. Carolyn often wished George had more time for her, but she enjoyed spending time with her girlfriends and, besides, if her plans worked out, she was about to become a very busy girl. *Yep,* she thought to herself, *Perhaps things are better left as they are. If George wants to spend a lot of time with his friends, I will have more time for work and study.* These thoughts made her feel better about the relationship, but she often wondered what it could mean in the long term.

Summer break passed quickly and it was time to start her junior year in high school. She promised herself to work extra hard this year. Who knows, perhaps a scholarship is not completely out of the question.

Her mother, Geraldine, soon learned the defense department sponsored a program called 'Stay in School' for high school juniors and seniors as well as college students. The program was designed to provide financial help to students wanting to earn money for college. Carolyn was soon interviewed by Colonel Lee at the Pentagon and hired as a GS-3 admin clerk. Fairfax high school, in turn, had placed her in their special 'college Prep' program allowing her to attend classes in the morning and go to work at the Pentagon in the afternoon. Her father, Cot, quickly realized she would need transportation. As an early birthday surprise, he had taken her car-shopping and bought a used 1955 Chevrolet. Jimmy and George had been well trained by their father in auto mechanics. Before she knew it, that used Chevy looked like it had just rolled off the assembly line. Carolyn was so proud!

Her junior year included studies in typing, shorthand, book-keeping, accounting, and algebra. Carolyn was devoted to her studies, anxious to apply what she learned in class to her work at the office. She was soon promoted to assistant secretary by her boss as her skills in typing and shorthand improved at an accelerated rate.*Hmm*, she often thought, *This admin stuff is easy. I wonder if all the other skills I need will be equally as easy to learn.* Her short-hand speed had climbed to 120 words per minute and her typing speed was getting close to ninety words per minute; she was fast and accurate.

It wasn't long before the staff at her office started saving work for her to do when she arrived after school. More and more often they would greet her as she came through the door with a pile of work they had saved for her and her alone. Without realizing it, her attention to detail coupled with an ever-evolving ability to confront and solve difficult problems in the work place were building a reputation for her that not many high school students enjoyed. Carolyn was a bright girl, mature beyond her teenage years; everyone around her knew she had the potential to rapidly climb the ladder of success in any field she would choose. She had success written all over her.

Her junior year passed quickly and before she knew it, summer was here again. She had finished the year with straight A's in every subject and enrolled in an English composition course at Northern Virginia Community College during the summer. The course was a night class, so she worked full time at the Pentagon during the day and attended class two nights a week for three hours.

Col Lee continued as her immediate supervisor and made it a point to introduce her to new work assignments with increasingly difficult challenges. *Someday, my dear, you will reach the top of your career ladder and who knows, you might be offering me a job before it's all over. In the meantime, I will try to make sure your beginning assignments and challenges build a sound base for long term success*, he thought to himself with a wry smile on his face.

"I need to improve my writing and composition skills," she told her mother. "The work I do at the office requires me to review composition of other staffers and while I can find their errors, I am not always sure why corrections are required. Perhaps this college-level course will help."

Geraldine was working as a secretary at a large defense agency and really understood Carolyn's concern.

"Anytime you take a college course to improve yourself, you benefit from the experience," Geraldine counseled. "You are a smart girl. Follow your instincts, you will be okay in the long run."

Each payday, Carolyn's paycheck was directly deposited in her savings account by the government. When the bank statement came in the mail at the end of each month, she would go over it with great pride in her accomplishment. A college education was getting closer with each payday that passed. Carolyn was motivated! *This is the right way to go about it*, she thought as she planned each financial step in her imagined college career.

During the summer, her relationship with George intensified. Other boys were interested, but George's good looks and charm were always just a little better than any of the others. He still did not spend his every available minute with her, but he did not pay attention to any other girl. Carolyn felt secure in the thought that George's affections were reserved for her and her alone. When she was not thinking about the office, her studies, or planning her college career, she wondered what life would be like if she were married to George. The thought gave her a warm feeling. George had hinted at marriage, but Carolyn paid little attention. She had an ambitious path before her and she was determined to follow her plan.

Her senior year at Fairfax High was hectic. School in the morning, work in the afternoon, and college classes at night. Going to bed early each evening was the only way she could make it through each long, tiring day. She saw George on the weekends, but he also was very busy. He was working as a part-time carpenter to make a little extra spending money while going to school. Jimmy told Peggy that George was quite good as a finishing carpenter and thought he would make a lot of money at it once he finished high school.

Carolyn continued taking college level courses at night school. Her boss, Col. Lee, enrolled her in a government program paying seventy-five percent of tuition and books for employees taking college level courses that were work related. Carolyn took courses in accounting, advanced English composition, creative writing, finance, business law, and a number of others suggested by her boss. Geraldine wondered if perhaps she might be carrying too much of a load, but Carolyn seemed to handle everything well.

"Oh well," Geraldine told Cot, "If it does become too much, we will see it and step in. In the meantime, we have a high school student who is earning her own living while paying for her college education all at the same time. Perhaps the hard work is good for her."

Cot was accustomed to hard work. He had been a carpenter all his life and knew the real meaning of long hours filled with hard work.

"I suppose you are right, dear," Cot had replied. "But I hope you will keep a close eye on her. She is much too young to allow her ambitions to run her into the ground," he said with a concerned look on his face.

As her senior year in high school drew to a close, Carolyn noted the absence of college offers. Her grades were very good, but not good enough to receive scholarship offers. On the other hand, Colonel Lee found her a full-time administrative position in the same defense agency where her mother worked.

"This agency is growing," he explained. "It has a mission that will only expand over the years. That means career opportunities for a bright girl like you will always be available. I have talked to a close friend of mine at the agency about you and he wants to talk with you about a full-time job." He continued. "His name is John Simmonds. I think you will like him a lot. In the not too distant future, I expect he will be one of the senior managers in the agency."

"Looks like decision time for me," Carolyn silently concluded.

"No college offers and not enough money in the bank to take on college as a full-time program" she quietly reasoned.

As if that wasn't enough, George had proposed! He wanted to get married right now. He had been offered a really good job at a very high salary.

"We can live real well with our two jobs," he proclaimed. "Let's get married now. We can live in an apartment for a while, save our money, and buy a nice house real soon." He had obviously given this matter a lot of thought.

Carolyn went over the alternatives and possibilities in her mind again and again, but in the end, she realized George was right. Both would have a good career, they would be happy together, and in the long run, their lives would only get better with time.

"Besides," she argued, "I can continue going to college at night and the government will pay the biggest part of it. That means the money I have saved can be used for other purposes." She reasoned.

"Not a bad plan," she concluded after going through the advantages and disadvantages once again.

The next day, she went out with George and announced she would accept his proposal. She would marry him! George was overjoyed.

Peggy and Jimmy had married in the summer before Carolyn started her senior year and they were doing very well. Jimmy was thinking about starting his own printing business and Peggy was saving every spare dollar she could get her hands on for a new house. Life was good!

George and Carolyn were married in the fall following graduation. She had accepted a job at the agency and it was doing extremely well. Her reputation within the agency for efficiency and effectiveness grew with every passing day. Without realizing it, she was making quite a name for herself. Col. Lee had made it a point to place her in a job under the care of his old friend, Mr. Simmonds, as an administrative assistant. *You have come a long way in a short time,* Mr. Simmonds often thought as he managed Carolyn's day-to-day activities. *Someday, you will be ready for bigger and better things, but for now, Col. Lee is correct, I need to build on the career base he started. Patience, my dear, patience,* Mr. Simmonds told himself.

The next morning, Mr. Simmonds stopped at Carolyn's desk and handed her an announcement.

"The agency is sponsoring career development courses for those who might be interested. This flyer announces two very important courses. One in advanced interpersonal skills and the other in facilitative leadership - a sociology based approach to meeting management. Both are great courses, sign up and let me know what the dates are. I think you will enjoy both of them."

He smiled at Carolyn and did not wait for an answer, he simply strolled out the door and down the hall to his next meeting.

"Yes sir," answered Carolyn, knowing he did not hear, but he knew she would comply.*He is really working hard to mentor my professional development,* Carolyn thought. *It's nice to have someone looking out for you.*

The years passed quickly. Robin Kay was born in the summer of 1964 and Michael William came along in the spring of 1967. Maternity leave turned into a full-time job as a wife and mother. She did not want to leave her job at the agency, but the demands of two small children made working full time seem an almost impossible task. At the same time, George had started his own business and was doing well. They bought a new home and the family settled in for the long term.

George's business demanded long hours every day. He was out of bed before dawn and often did not return home until late in the evening. His weekends were spent preparing for the business week to come. If there was any spare time, George preferred to spend it with his male friends at the local bar and grill. Their time together was extremely limited.

Carolyn was always busy, but missed her work at the agency. The routines of meetings, conferences, and all the duties association with her work held a magnetic attraction for her, but she especially missed the interaction with other employees. For now, however, taking care of the children and her home were much higher priorities. She was lonely a lot, but the routine of a Mom and housewife kept her busy enough to occupy each day. George and Carolyn often talked about the absence of quality time together, but never quite came up with a plan to change the trend.

Carolyn observed, "It seems like the older we get, the farther apart we become. Our interests are becoming very different. Perhaps maturity is taking us in different directions?"

George did not like these discussions. He knew he was increasingly unhappy, but could not figure out how to solve the problem. As luck would have it, time made everything better. Before long, both children were in school. The need for Carolyn to stay at home all day, every day, had passed.

"It's time for me to go back to work," she told George.

"The extra money will help and perhaps working will help improve our relationship," she said wishfully.

"I will update my resume and give it to Mom, perhaps the agency still has a place for me," she commented with a gleam of hope in her eye.

For the next two weeks, Carolyn worked continuously to get her resume re-written and typed. Finally, she gave it to Geraldine.

"I'm ready to go back to work," she told her mother. "Time for me to start earning my keep!"

Geraldine was pleased her daughter had decided to continue her career. She knew Carolyn had a lot of promise and wanted to see her get back on the road to reaching her full potential.

"All right, dear," Geraldine replied, "I will take this to the agency and see if there is anything available."

For the next two weeks, Carolyn was on pins and needles as she waited for a response. Then, one afternoon as she finished a writing assignment in economics for her night class at Northern Virginia Community College, the phone rang.

The voice at the other end was Geraldine.

"Hi, sweetie," she said. "How about a job interview tomorrow morning?" she asked.

"Everything is all arranged at the agency. I will pick you up at 7:00 AM on my way to work and take you to the interview. Put on your best dress and I will see you then," Geraldine ordered.

"Wait!" replied Carolyn "Who am I interviewing with, what is the job, what is the grade and salary?" she sputtered.

"No time for all that sweetie," Geraldine replied, "Just be ready tomorrow morning, I think you will like what is being offered."

Carolyn could hardly sleep that night. *I will be a nervous wreck at this rate,* she thought.

When George's alarm went off at 4:30, she had more than enough of the tossing and turning routine. She jumped out of bed and started getting ready.

"Need plenty of time to hide the dark circles under my eyes from lack of sleep," She moaned.

By the time Geraldine arrived, Carolyn had gone through a dozen introductory speeches, answered what seemed like a million imagined questions, and felt confident she was ready.

The ride to the agency was quiet. Every time Carolyn asked about the interview, Geraldine would avoid the question with a hand wave and a "You'll see" response.

They finally arrived, parked the car, and walked into the agency. Carolyn was issued a visitor badge and Geraldine escorted her to a waiting room on the second floor.

"I'll let them know you are here, sweetie," she remarked, then walked away without another word.

Carolyn sat down and began to go over her introductory speech again. As she gazed at her hands, folded in her lap, she noticed someone walking toward her out of the corner of her eye. As she looked up, her eyes came to rest on a most familiar face.

"Mr. Simmonds!" she exclaimed and she rose to greet him.

"Carolyn," he said with a gentle smile. "Thank you for coming in. I need a Secretary and you are it! Your desk is ready, your grade is a GS-6, and your security clearance has been reinstated. You start immediately. Any questions?" he gently inquired with a wide grin.

"No sir, yes sir, as you might guess, I only have about a million-and-one questions," she replied.

"Fine. I guessed as much," Mr. Simmonds replied. "Since I last saw you, I have climbed the ladder of success and am now the Deputy Director for Resource Management. I stay really busy these days. I have a meeting to attend and am in a bit of a rush, I will take you to security for your permanent badge, from there, you have to go to personnel to do all that new employee paperwork, you know the way. I'll meet you in the office sometime around noon and we can talk about the office and your new job. We can also discuss resumption of your career. Welcome back, at last," he smiled. "I always hoped you would come back - often asked your mother if you had changed your mind," he said with a wide grin.

"I can't tell you how happy I was when she told me you wanted to come back. Off we go!" he exclaimed as he motioned for her to walk with him to the security office.*I'm on my way*, Carolyn thought to herself as she joined him and walked along the busy corridor.*Looks like someday finally arrived*, Mr. Simmonds thought as he made his way down the busy hallway.

Chapter III

Carolyn quickly learned she was a perfect match for the new job. Most of the first day was filled with new employee orientation. Quickly, after settling into the routine of the new job, she was pleased to find many of the employees working in this office she knew during her first term with the agency. To her delight, many of the senior staff officers working for Mr. Simmonds were friends she made during her first term who had climbed the ladder to success during her absence.

"Take a day or so to get acquainted with our staff and remembering your way around the agency. Then, we will get down to business," Mr. Simmonds told her at the end of her first day. *A job isn't supposed to be this much fun*, Carolyn thought to herself as she organized her working area and made the small office a bit more like home. *I suppose once the newness wears off, it will be just another job*, she imagined. But that was not to be the case. At her first staff meeting, Mr. Simmonds announced that Carolyn would not only fill the role of his personal secretary, but function as his Executive Office manager as well.

"For a long time, we have been looking for someone who could take charge of the administrative functions of our division," Mr. Simmonds said.

"We wanted someone who would assume responsibility for all the admin tasks and functions, tell each of us where we fitted into that role, and see to it the admin system worked for us," he announced.

"Well, I am pleased to tell you that we have found our Girl Friday," he said with obvious pride as he stared at Carolyn.

"Carolyn and I worked together in the past and many of you know her from the days she worked part-time. I will expect you to fill her in on how your piece of the puzzle fits the big picture. In the meantime, welcome aboard Carolyn, we are all delighted you have joined us," he concluded with an expression of obvious relief.

Mr. Simmonds' organization was filled with resource managers. They managed financial and personnel resources for the agency and none of them liked the additional workload associated with administration. Their previous Office Manager had been very good, but she had moved to another organization where she was promoted into a first-level management position. Now, Carolyn had the job of not only learning the many routines associated with this organization, but trying to find a way to be even better at the job than her predecessor. The staff was more than helpful. Each of them worked closely with Carolyn to help her understand their function, then explain how she could support them to make their jobs even better and, perhaps, easier. Clearly, they were happy she had come along to take over the burden of administration. Carolyn was a good student and learned the requirements of each of their positions. To improve her depth of understanding, she reviewed their individual job descriptions to make sure she understood the scope of their duties and responsibilities. This information might come in handy later as she applied the administrative functions of the organization to each of their roles.

Carolyn's effectiveness was felt almost immediately. More and more each day, the staff's dependence on her to not only provide the necessary administrative support, but anticipate their needs in advance and have everything in readiness when the time came, grew with leaps and bounds. The great part of it was that Carolyn's understanding of each job function within the organization grew with each passing day. Her ability to anticipate job requirements of the staff, with great depth, made her more and more valuable to each of the staff officers working their day-to-day functions. Once she had the office under control, she began to expand her contacts to other administrators throughout the agency. Over time, her network grew to the point where she could get almost anything needed by the people in her office with a single phone call. In return, she made sure she was more than immediately responsive when someone outside her office asked for help. Before long, the routine within her office was running like a well-oiled machine. Carolyn's reputation within the agency as the one to go to when you needed help grew and grew with every passing day.

Unfortunately, successes achieved on the home-front were not as great as those at the office. George's work started before the sun came up every day and did not end until long after sunset. More often than not, he came home late each evening, just in time to say goodnight to the kids, eat dinner, take a quick shower, then off to bed. His weekends were filled with family related chores such as taking care of the house and lawn, shopping with Carolyn for the family, with an occasional social visit to someone in the family. Almost every available minute of every day was programmed well in advance which resulted in a very busy schedule for him. Carolyn soon found herself caught-up in the same frenzy that seemed to overwhelm George. The commute to and from the office was one hour each way - traffic was always bumper-to-bumper. At least ten hours of each week day were filled with her job. As responsibility and dependency grew, she found it necessary to linger an hour or two at the office each day to make sure everything was under control. While she did not regret the long hours, the fact that her job now occupied at least twelve hours of each week day did not make things easier at home.

Time passed quickly. Weeks and months seemed to dissolve in a blur as time moved at a frenzied pace. Before she knew it, the new job was two years old. She had been promoted twice and the number of awards for efficiency and productivity filled the walls of her office. She had managed to continue her education by taking night courses at the local community college, but the emphasis in her life was job and family. Every evening she fell into bed exhausted while her mind wildly ran through events anticipated in the next day.

Robin and Mike seemed to have risen above the fast-paced lifestyles of their parents. Both were doing well in school and seemed to be happy and content. George and Carolyn somehow found time to fit school and social events of the children into their hectic schedules, but there was very little time for each other.

It seemed clear to Carolyn the interests she once shared with George no longer existed. The carefree, easy going lifestyle they once enjoyed was gone. Carolyn's interests moved more toward the intellectual side of her personality that had developed by leaps and bounds since she started taking college courses and working in an environment where almost everyone held advance degrees.

Her day at the office was filled with the tasks of everyday business, but there was always time for intellectual discussions such as off-Broadway theater, literature, politics, business finance, and international affairs. She was pleased to find herself able to hold her own in conversations involving economics, politics, and international business; those night courses were paying off in more ways than one. While those in her business environment held bachelor and master's degrees in various disciplines, they almost always tried to include her in discussions of complex social and political issues, genuinely interested in her views and opinions.

George's interests seemed to focus on a much different lifestyle. Watching a football game on the weekends with his buddies, frequent trips to watch stock car races punctuated with an occasional 'happy hour' at the local bar were the pursuits that held George's interests.

During one of her annual performance report interviews, Mr. Simmonds suggested if she continued her education and was able to complete the bachelor degree program, he had no doubt she would, someday, be a strong contender for his position.

"You have the natural instincts of an executive manager, now all you need is a bit more professional experience, a solid foundation of formal education to back it up and, for you, the sky is the limit. But, even without the degree, I have no doubt you will be extremely successful in your career. I am very interested to see where your career will take you over the next fifteen to twenty years and I intend to drive that train as much as I can," he commented.

The months and years passed quickly as Carolyn and George continued through their very busy, but separate, lives. They were drifting farther and farther apart and neither could find a way to close the ever-widening gap between them. Carolyn's career improved with every passing day. Just when she thought things could not be better professionally, Mr. Simmonds called her into his office and announced that she was ready for the next career step.

"I know you like your job here and, frankly, you are the best I have ever seen at it, but I see an opportunity to help you become the professional I know you are capable of becoming. Colonel Henderson, head of our civilian and military personnel division, needs an Executive Officer. It is a GS-9 slot.," he explained. "My intention is to transfer you into that position with an automatic promotion. Colonel Henderson cannot believe my generosity, but I have an ulterior motive," he continued.

"Placing you in this position solves a few problems for our organization. For you, it is a promotion! At the same time, it will fill a hole in your resource management experience that will help prepare you for the future. This all fits nicely with the fact that I have expanded Colonel Henderson's responsibilities in the civilian and military personnel arena which includes several challenges that are right up your alley. He will need the help only you can provide if he is to succeed. Keep in mind, Carolyn, you remain in the resource management family and still work for me, indirectly as it may be, and when the time comes, we will be talking more about your future in this agency," he finished with a big smile.

"Any questions?" he asked.

"No sir," Carolyn replied. "I just want to thank you for being so good to me and trying to guide my career in the right direction," she smiled "I will call Colonel Henderson and arrange the transfer. I will miss you and the staff," she confided as she walked out of the room.

Mr. Simmonds watched her walk away. As she disappeared down the hallway, he looked down at his desk top and whispered under his breath, "You won't be gone long, my dear. Someday, when you are ready, I will bring you back for bigger and better things. Someday you will be a senior leader in this agency, if I have my way."

Within a week, Carolyn reported to Colonel Henderson, ready to go to work. Then they sat down for the orientation discussion. Colonel Henderson was an impressive army officer. He was much younger than one might expect a Colonel to be with only a hint of greying hair and so many decorations on his uniform that they reached all the way to the top of his left shoulder. He was a fine-looking officer with a solid reputation as one who can get things done.

"You will be my Executive Officer," Col. Henderson began, "and I suspect that will be no easy chore as I tend to be a bit disorganized and depend a great deal on my XO to make sure I am properly focused. Of course, you already know I work for Mr. Simmonds and you also know Lt .Col. Scarsdale is head of the Military Personnel Division and Mr. Ward heads our Civilian Personnel Division, both working for me," he said as he looked up from his desk.

"I suppose," he continued, "You need little introduction to our personnel or the work we do since you always seemed to have such a keen understanding of who we are and what we need to get the job done. It seems to me, the only question I need answered is why in the world would Mr. Simmonds let you go?"

Col Henderson's brow was wrinkled as a questioning expression covered his face.

"I can only tell you what he told me," Carolyn replied.

"He said I need the experience," she continued with a smile.

"He also said you needed help down here and I was well suited to provide that support, so, here I am," she replied with a look of confidence.

"That's good enough for me," Col. Henderson replied with a smile.

"Everyone in this agency knows you were the force that made this directorate work so well. I want you to do for me what you did for Mr. Simmonds and that task may not be as simple as it sounds. But, in a few words, I want you to take charge and get my staff working as well as you did for Mr. Simmonds. Can you do that?" he asked with a boyish look on his face.

"Yes sir," Carolyn replied. "I will do as you wish."

"One more thing," Col. Henderson remarked as he stood up, "I am bringing in a new deputy for Mr. Ward. His responsibilities on the civilian side of the house are about to take a bug jump, so I think he will need some help; I will brief you on the details later. Additionally, Mr. Simmonds has indicated we need to do a better job managing our joint-service military enlisted work force. To get that taken care of I have selected Master Sergeant Jim Knight. He is currently assigned to our Hawaii office, but I have asked him to come back to the headquarters to work for me. I have known him for many, many years. I think you will find him to be very different from the typical army Sergeant. The two of you will be working very closely together; I think you have much in common. I will introduce you as soon as he arrives, next month. I have a feeling the two of you will make a great team!" he said with a big smile. "Again, I will brief you on the details soon as Mr. Simmonds and I work out the basic focus of the job."

Col Henderson moved around his desk, held out his hand saying, "Welcome aboard, Carolyn, I am pleased you accepted the assignment."

He shook her hand and motioned for her to walk out of his office with him.

"Your office is on the left, next to mine," he said as he walked away. "Weekly staff meeting is 9:00 AM each Monday morning and oh, by the way, congratulations on your promotion, I know it was well deserved. Bye now, going up to see Mr. Simmonds."

Carolyn walked into her new office and began getting everything organized.*Hmmm,* she thought, *I hope he won't be upset when I tell him I have a week of vacation approved for next month. George and I need some time to ourselves to try and patch-up our failing marriage.*

For a brief moment, she became lost in her thoughts of how to salvage her ever failing marriage, but quickly brought herself back to the task at hand. Carolyn made a note to inform her new boss about the vacation and went about her business of getting ready for the next step in her career. Looking down at her desk, she saw a folder labeled "Master Sergeant Jim Knight." She opened the file noticing documents labeled "Personal background".*Hmm,* she thought, *Guess I better get up to speed on this one real fast.*

As the thumbed through the documents in the file she noted letters of commendation from a three-star general, a rather impressive Bronze Star recommendation from a tour in Vietnam, and a number of other documents talking about accomplishment of a then Major Henderson and a Staff Sergeant Jim Knight.

"My, my," she mumbled, "This young sergeant does get around. I bet he is a very interesting person."

Carolyn closed the file and placed it on the corner of her desk for future reference. *More on this later,* she thought. *Now it is time to concentrate on another interesting person; his name is George.*

The days passed quickly as Carolyn busied herself with details of her new job and plans for her vacation with George. Colonel Henderson informed her that he already knew about her planned vacation and had arranged for a temporary assistant to fill in during her absence. Now all she had to do was figure out a way to bring her and George back together. That was going to be a formidable task because she was no longer really sure George really wanted to continue.

Chapter IV

Jim Knight sat on the front steps of his parents' home, waiting for his friends to finish lunch so they could fill the afternoon with basketball. It was a warm 1953 summer day, perfect for basketball and fun with friends. Summer vacation from school had been great, Jim had counted every day of the school year as he waited for summer vacation to arrive. At 12 years old, he was not a good student and did only enough to get by. Somewhere in the back of his mind, he thought education might be important, but he was not really sure why. Only one of his cousins had attended college but, for the most part, either a job in construction or one at the local ship yard seemed to be the choices guiding most local males. With the exception of his Dad and Uncle Kirk, who had chosen careers in the military, it seemed his future was already predetermined. For these reasons, more emphasis was placed on social activities and less on academic achievement.*All I need to do is bring home straight C's on my report card; Mom and Dad will leave me alone*, He thought to himself. *School is okay, but no fun at all.*

Jim's Dad, Jimmy, worked at the air force base as an aircraft mechanic. That, along with his retirement from the air force allowed the family to live comfortably. His younger brother,

Russell was five years his junior and Roslyn, the baby of the family, was four years behind Russell.

Their mother, Eloise, had worked while Jimmy was on active duty with the air force, but now that he had retired and the family was certain to stay in one place for a long while, she stayed home and took care of the family. All things considered, life was very good for the Knight clan.

Carman Vincent and Sharon Harris came walking down the street, each bouncing a basketball in front of them.

"You guys ready for the big game?" Carman asked. "We think it is time for the girls against the boys," she boasted.

"In the first place, I think there will be more boys than girls today," Jim responded belligerently.

"If Aaron brings his two brothers, Jackie and Dee, there will be four boys, and if Trevor shows up, you will really be outnumbered, unless you have some help I don't know about.," Jim quipped.

"Oh, really?" replied Sharon, "We thought only you and Aaron were playing."

"Tell you what," Carman said, thoughtfully, "At the end of the game we will compare the points scored by each of the girls with each of the boys. If either of the girls score more points than any one of the boys, you buy ice cream for a week. If we lose, we buy the ice cream."

A big smile crossed her face.

"Okay, you have a deal. You two are good, but not that good.," Jim responded as he jumped to his feet and joined the girls walking toward the basketball court.

Jim knew somewhere in the back of his memory that individually the boys always lost to the girls, but he had a paper route and could afford to accept the wager.

Jim, Aaron, Trevor, Carman, and Sharon were very close friends. There was a lot of competitive spirit between them, but together they were a formidable team in any sport, especially basketball and football. Both Sharon and Carman were tall and slender. Carman had a twenty- foot, turn-around jump-shot that was a certain score nine-out-of-ten times while Sharon's hook shot was as good or better than most of the boys in school. Both girls played football as well as any of the boys and could catch a pass downfield in almost any situation. In this group all were equals and each was very protective of the others; they were very close friends.

Carman was the good student. She made straight As in everything. Sharon ran a close second, but academically, the boys were all running along the same path of achievement; Cs were the norm and should an occasional B or A show up on the report card, others in the tight-knit group would hear about it for a very long time. But, good grades for the boys were an exception, not the rule.

The big social event of each week was Friday night at the youth center on the air force base because the father of each of them was retired military, all of them were allowed to attend youth functions on the local air force base. Each Friday evening at 5:00 an air force bus came to the neighborhood and carried all the kids to the youth center for a night of movies, popcorn, and all kinds of games thought-up by the adult chaperones. It was a lot of fun for all!

The teenagers really had a bad deal, in Jim's mind. Their night was Saturday. The bus brought them to the youth center, but all the teens called it "The Teen Club". Their night was filled with dancing, watching TV, and playing pool.*Yuk*, thought Jim, *Why would anybody want to spend an evening dancing with girls? I don't understand that at all. Bet they wish they could watch movies like we do!* he often thought.

Clearly, his male hormones had not started the process that would eventually focus his attention on the opposite sex. For now, his view of girls and boys was pretty much defined by their ability to play basketball, football, or baseball, and often tipped in favor of the best athlete.

The summer passed quickly and the following school year dragged by, day by day. Jim struggled to keep his grades at an acceptable level, while Carman was at the other extreme. She easily continued the great grades; she was at the top of her class. *I suppose some of us are just naturally smarter than others*, Jim reasoned. *I bet Carman will eventually go on to college while the rest of us try to figure out what lies ahead. I must not be real bright. If I were, school would not be so difficult*, he reasoned.

The school year passed and summer arrived right on schedule. The group of kids continued their routine like it had been scripted for them in advance. Sports during the day with a big reward each Friday evening filled with movies and popcorn. Jim thought the world was a great place to be and all was good. But, as all good things tend to do, the end came abruptly.

During the late summer, all of them had their thirteenth birthday. To their disappointment, Friday night at the youth center was out. They were no longer eligible to attend the Friday night movie party. Now they were all teenagers and only had a choice of going to the Saturday night teen dance party or staying home. Their first dance party was, for each of them, a very tense evening.

Soon as they arrived, the music started and all the other kids moved onto the dance floor. Jim's group stood on the sidelines watching in wonder as the kids on the dance floor went around and around in time to the music. Jim had started taking trumpet lessons in junior high school and was doing well. His sense of rhythm was good, but his feet did not know where to go.

"Do you have any idea how to dance?" Carman asked Jim.

"No ma'am," Jim replied.

"Where do you learn to do this stuff and how do you know which dance to do?" he asked.

Aaron tapped his finger against the side of his head as he thought about it. Finally, he reasoned.

"I think they have dance lessons here on Saturday afternoon. Do you think we should attend?" he asked of the group.

"Forget that," Trevor responded. "Giving up my Saturday night is one thing, but I am not giving up our ball games just so I can learn to dance with a girl," he stammered.

"Yeah, why would anybody want to do that," Sharon offered with a gleam in her eye. "It would be much more fun to stay home, play basketball, then tell all your friends how the girls beat you by a ton," she sarcastically replied with her hands on her hips.

The big smile on Trevor's face disappeared as Sharon's meaning began to take form in his brain.

Jim and the girls were tall and slender, but Trevor was quite the opposite. He was a bit short, slightly overweight, and a bit awkward on his feet anywhere except on a football field. He knew his chances of becoming a graceful dancer were slim!

"Welcome to our dance party," came a small voice from the darkness behind them.

Lorraine Nash walked out of the shadows with a big smile on her face and joined the group.

Lorraine had spent a lot of time working with Jim in their math class. If it had not been for her, he probably would have failed the subject more than once. Lorraine was about six months older than Jim, so she had started coming to the Saturday evening dance event a lot sooner than any of them. She was a lot like Carman; tall, slender, graceful, and wore her auburn hair short. She was an excellent student. All-in-all, Lorraine was a very nice person, but she lived on the other side of town, so they only saw her at school.

Jim turned to face Lorraine and responded, "Thanks Lorraine! This is our first night here. We are kinda trying to figure out how all this works."

"Do you know how to dance?" Lorraine asked.

"No," Trevor responded. "All of us have two left feet and they never go in the right direction unless a football is involved."

"Believe me," Lorraine replied with a big smile, "I know exactly how you feel. When I started coming here a few months ago, I was lost, but my big sister Jackie taught me the basics. It isn't as hard as it looks," she said as she looked up at Jim.

Lorraine reached out, took Jim by the hand, and before he knew it, they were standing close together in the middle of the dance floor. Jim had never been this close to a girl his age except when playing football or basketball.

"Lightly hold my right hand with your left, place your right hand on my back, like this," she instructed as they moved close together. "Now, take one small step with each beat of the music, four steps forward, then four steps backward.," she offered.

"Then what?" Jim asked with a sheepish look on his face.

"Then do it all over again," Lorraine replied. "It is not as difficult as you might think, just start with your left foot and let your hips sway with the rhythm of the music," she said giving him a slight tug.Jim followed Lorraine's instructions to the letter. Much to his surprise, the hard part was over before it started; one, two, three, four forward, then one, two, three, four, backward. Simple!

The slow song ended, another one started, and Lorraine kept Jim on the dance floor. When it was over, she held his hand tightly as they walked back to the group.

"Welcome back Arthur and Kathryn Murray," Trevor quipped "You two looked smooth as glass."

As Lorraine started walking away, she looked back over her shoulder saying, "Keep practicing Jim and I'll see you here next week."

Sharon placed her arm around Jim's shoulder, pulled him close so no one else could hear, and whispered in his ear, "Looks like she is sweet on you, big boy."

Jim gently pulled away and brushed his long blond hair out of his eyes trying to look as casual as he could.

"That wasn't hard at all, don't know why they make such a big deal out of it," he said confidently, trying to smile as casually as he could.

But a little voice in the back of his head was saying things he had not heard before. As Lorraine walked away, he noticed how tightly her skirt clung to her slender, shapely hips and while he was dancing with her, he could not help but notice how nice that low cut, tight sweater looked on her. Jim wasn't sure what had happened, but that little voice kept telling him the change he had just experienced was just the beginning and would, over time, magically change his life, forever!

Trevor noticed a strange look on Jim's face and a gleam in his emerald green eyes.

"Remind me not to dance with girls anytime soon, it looks too confusing to be any fun," Trevor remarked.

Jim smiled weakly because he knew Trevor's choice of words had hit the nail right on the head. *Confusing*, he thought to himself, *is an understatement.*

Jim's experience on the dance floor with Lorraine must have been contagious because it seemed like no time at all before Aaron started dating a girl named Cathy. Carman and Roland Bridges became a common sight. Sharon and Trevor held the line for more basketball and less dancing, but both knew they were fighting a losing battle. It would not be long before the team that had been so competitive on the field of sports would become more and more so on the dance floor.

The months quickly passed. Almost overnight, high school became the new test of the day for Jim. Music continued to be the only subject he handled well. During interstate musical competition, Jim and his high school trumpet trio won third place in state-wide competition.

He was selected to play in the school dance band and all was well with the trumpet. Music was his strongest subject in school, but it was everything else associated with school that made life difficult. But Jim was no dummy. He worked hard enough to get by in school, but what would happen in his life after school worried him more and more as time passed.

Music seemed to help the romantic side of life move a bit faster for Jim. Soon he met Ann Carver and they seemed to hit it off right away. She lived on the other side of town, but the public bus system made it easy to visit each other. Ann's father, Edward, was on active duty with the air force, so she was a regular at the Saturday evening dance. Before long, neither ever danced with anyone else. More and more, they spent as much time together as they could.

For Jim, Ann was a source of motivation. She was an excellent student, so Jim worked a bit harder to keep up with her. As his academic track record began to improve, he thought more and more about the importance of a college education. His music teacher suggested he consider application to a school of music, but that seemed too much of a long shot. Jim knew he was a fair musician, but not good enough to be truly successful. There had to be another way.

"If you really want to go to college, I will make it happen," his dad told him. "But you will need to work harder on subjects other than music."

The thought was comforting, but Russell and Roslyn were straight A students and if any of his father's hard-earned wages were to go for education, it should go to the two children most deserving.*Besides,* Jim thought, *I may not be smart enough to make it through college, then all that money would be wasted.*

If my family is willing to spend money on education, they should spend it on a sure thing, he reasoned. *Dad doesn't have a lot of money to waste and my brother and sister are a sure success while I am a real long shot. There has to be another way.*

The high school years passed slowly. Each day was a real challenge, but Jim kept pace and, thanks to tutoring from Ann, held his own. In his senior year, Trevor announced that he had joined the army and would be leaving soon after graduation. Jim was completely caught off guard.

"Why in the world would you join the army?" Jim asked as he and Trevor walked home from the bus stop after school.

"Because," Trevor responded, "My dad can't afford to send me to college. So my plan says, I join the army for three years and make them send me to a good technical school. Then I have two or three years to work that new trade and really learn it well while I am on active duty. At the end of the three-year enlistment, I am discharged from the army and they will pay for my college education. It's called the G.I. bill. You should look into it, because your dad can't afford to send you to school any more than mine can!" Trevor said, grinning from ear to ear.

It seemed clear he had given this idea a great deal of thought. Trevor's plan was simple and reasonable. *Wow*, Jim thought, *and besides all that, they pay you a salary while you are in the army.* He made a mental note to talk to his dad about the military. *After all, Dad spent twenty years in the military. This could be the solution to all my problems. I wonder what Ann will think of all this?*

To his surprise, his father was receptive to the idea.

"It is not uncommon for a young man to join the military as part of the growing-up process. If you don't know what you want to do, join the army, go to a good trade school, travel, practice a good technical skill, and see some of the world you live in. I would suggest you consider telecommunications as a career field; that seems to be the coming thing. Then, if you do not want to make a career of the military, get out and you should have no problem finding a good paying job in your technical skill," his father wisely counseled.

When he discussed the idea with Ann, her response left him speechless.

"I like it," she said with a big smile. "I like it a lot. In fact, with you in the army, earning a salary, and able to take care of

yourself, we could get married!"

"Married?" Jim repeated weakly "You mean you and me, married?"

"Yep," Ann replied "You have a problem with that? You do intend to marry me, don't you?" she asked firmly.

Jim's head was spinning. He had considered a lot of possibilities, but marriage? *Is that what I should do*? he silently asked himself

"Oh yes, yes," he replied, quickly recovering his thoughts, "I just wasn't sure you were that serious about me."

"In case you haven't noticed," she replied, "We have been together longer than any of our friends. It only seems natural that we would want to make it permanent," she explained.

Jim knew he was not ready to take on the responsibilities of a wife and family; he was still struggling to get through high school. But, on the other hand, Ann made a good point. He could not imagine being with anyone else but her. His mind was spinning as he tried to collected his thoughts and respond.

"Okay, okay," Jim replied with a stern, knowing look on his face, "I agree, we should do that, but there are a few things we need to do first."

"For example?" Ann asked

"Well," he started with a serious, knowing look on his face,

"First, we finish school, then I will join the army. I will need a year or so before they will allow me to get married," he explained.

"In the meantime," he continued, "you can either go to college or get a job to save some money so we can set-up housekeeping."

He looked into her eyes hoping his plan made good sense to her.

She stared back at him for the longest time as she went over the details in her mind. Suddenly a big smile came across her face as everything fell into place.

"Okay," she said with a big smile, "We will use the first year after graduation to get on our collective feet, then we will get married and live together."

"Yes ma'am," Jim replied. "By then we will have everything in place," he explained with visible relief.

They soon announced the plan to their parents. While the usual exchange about being much too young was predictable, in the end, both sets of parents arrived at the same conclusion: They agree to wait for at least a year. In real time, that is about eighteen months from now. A lot can happen in eighteen months.

While a bit uncomfortable at first, Jim soon became accustomed to the idea and started planning in earnest. More and more, the idea that the two of them would be together for all time seemed more and more appealing.

The remaining school year passed quickly. Carman received a scholarship to Penn State University. Aaron's family announced they would be moving to Missouri immediately after graduation and Sharon announced plans to marry her longtime boyfriend, Greg. Trevor and Jim were off to the army. Almost overnight, the group that had gone through childhood together set out on paths that would rarely cross again as they went through life. While none of them realized it, their childhood was gone. From this day forward, they would become young adults; the music they heard coming silently from their deepest thoughts would be unlike any they had ever experienced before.

Chapter V

Before he knew it, Jim was at Fort Jackson, South Carolina for basic training. Now he was a private in the U.S. Army. The new adventure had begun. On the day he left home, his father sat down with him for what he would remember as the only serious father-to-son talk in their entire relationship.

"For you," his dad began, "This is truly a new beginning. Everything you do, from this day forward, will color and influence the rest of your life. If you have ever considered becoming serious about anything in your life, now is the time. Make every event a learning experience. Learn to apply the lessons you will receive and work hard to learn every lesson better than anyone else. Finally, and this is the most important, always, always be the best at what you do," his father counseled.

At the bus station. he hugged his mother and told her not to worry.

When he shook his dad's hand, his father pulled him closed and whispered in his ear, "The things you learn in army basic training may someday be the lessons that will save your life and the lives of others if you ever have to go to war. Learn well, son. I think you will find it isn't a bad life at all."

Jim smiled at his father and moved toward the bus.

As he walked up the steps of the bus, he looked over his shoulder to see an unmistakable wink in his father's eye. For the first time in as long as he could remember, Jim felt confident he had made the right decision and chosen the best path to his future.*The path to tomorrow*, he thought to himself. *I will take your advice, Dad*, he silently promised as he walked toward an empty seat. *Today, I am a new person, everything has changed. This is a new beginning!*

After a short trip to the recruiting center in Richmond for swearing in, physical exams, and preparation of his new army record set, the train trip to Ft. Jackson passed quickly. A short bus ride from the train station delivered Jim and an entire bus load of wide-eyed recruits to their new home for the next two months - all were ready to begin the new adventure in their lives.

As the bus rolled to a stop in front of an older frame building, Jim saw an impressive army sergeant standing by the door of a small building watching the bus as it came to a stop as if at his command. Everyone filed off the bus as the sergeant came closer to them. The sergeant motioned them to form lines in front of him until there were four lines, one in front of the other. He then divided them into four separate groups and held his hand above his head.

"Quiet please," he ordered. His voice was deep and firm. There was no doubt, he was not accustomed to repeating himself.

"My name is First Sergeant Franklin," he said firmly.

"You have no idea what that means right now, but over the next eight weeks, you will learn. In the meantime, I think it sufficient to say I am the one ultimately in charge of your little worlds. Work hard, learn well, do what you are told, when you are told, and you will not see much of me. On the other hand, start screwing around, and you will see a lot of me and I promise you, it will not be fun."

First Sergeant Franklin placed his hands on his hips, moved closer to the formation and spoke firmly "Now, gentlemen, let's get down to business."

His green dress uniform was immaculate.

Every seam in place and well pressed. His height appeared to be around 6'4" and he was in excellent physical condition. His barrel chest, slender waist and crew-cut hair made him appear as a model for an army recruiting poster; he was impressive to look at. The ribbons on his left chest started above the left pocket and rose to the top of his shoulder.

Jim was impressed and amazed by the image of this army sergeant. *This army First Sergeant is the most impressive individual I have ever seen. He will be my role model*, Jim thought as he committed the image of First Sergeant Franklin to permanent memory.

The next eight weeks passed faster than any timeframe Jim ever remembered. Each day started promptly at 4:00AM and did not end until the end of daily inspections at 10:30 PM. Each day was filled with classes and practical exercises on army procedures and practices. The recruits learned how to wear their uniforms, were trained in hand-to-hand combat, attended endless classes on military weapons and topped the classroom lectures off with actual exercises in firing weapons, negotiating combat simulated battlefields, and last, but certainly not least, physical conditioning all day, every day. After eight weeks of intensive training, Jim felt better and more confident that he ever had. Through it all, Jim had become nearly obsessed with the qualities of military leadership. He continually questioned his training sergeant about being in charge, combat leadership, and decision making. He was determined to fully understand the leadership process so that when the time came, he could apply his lessons effectively.

On his last day of basic training, he was preparing to board a bus which would take him from Ft. Jackson to Ft Gordon, Georgia, seventy-five miles away, for communications school. As Jim was waiting to board the bus, First Sergeant Franklin appeared out of nowhere. He motioned for Jim to join him. Jim quickly moved in front of the First Sergeant, standing at rigid attention.

"Yes, First Sergeant," he said firmly trying to hide his nervousness.

"Relax young man," the First Sergeant replied. "I wanted to stop by to say goodbye and pass along a small piece of advice that may be useful to you."

"Have I done something wrong First Sergeant?" Jim asked with a sinking feeling in the pit of his stomach.

"No, no, not at all," the First Sergeant replied. "In fact, it's quite the opposite. I have watched you closely during your stay here. I see an aggressive, intelligent young soldier who is eager to learn and anxious to become a productive member of the military family. You have all the qualities we look for in our future leaders and in you, I see me fifteen or twenty years ago. The advice I have for you is this," he said with a grin on his chiseled face.

"Do not allow anyone to discourage you. You have a quick mind, you learn fast, and are able to grasp complex detail quickly; that is a rare quality in one so young.," he said.

"Do not," he said emphatically, "allow anyone to tell you that you aren't smart enough to learn and perform at the highest levels and secondly, do not allow anyone to lower your standards. You are a bright, aggressive young man and once your lessons are complete, you will be a leader of tomorrow."

His face suddenly became stern and his voice lowered. He folded his hand and poked Jim in the chest with his finger saying, "Finally, and perhaps most important of all, when you get to your first permanent assignment after communications school, get your ass in night school. The leader of tomorrow will be one who is well educated, well trained, and experienced. The army will take care of the training and experience you need to become an effective leader; you must take care of the education. You will not be able to succeed in the army of tomorrow without a college degree. Your officers will all be college educated, make sure you are their intellectual equal. When you reach that point, their reliance on you and trust in you will propel you to the highest levels of success."

The First Sergeant held out his hand, offering a handshake. "I see the question on your face," the first sergeant offered. "Yes, I took my own advice; I just finished my master's degree and I expect you to do the same."

Jim was totally surprised; he took the First Sergeant's hand with a weak smile and said in a low voice, "Thank you First Sergeant, I will not let you down."

First Sergeant Franklin pumped his hand, smiled, and replied "I know you won't. Welcome to the army son."

The First Sergeant turned on his heel and was gone, but the motivational forces he set in motion would continue to work over the entire lifetime of a young soldier from Virginia.

Communications school was almost too easy for Jim. He was at the top of the graduating class. Jim had decided to become not just a good student, but among the best. Each evening after class, he took advantage of the study sessions offered by the instructors. His spare time was spent going over his class notes and making sure he had a full understanding of the lessons taught in the classroom. Eight weeks later, when the course was finished, Jim was assigned to Ft. Meade, Maryland - his first permanent assignment. Now, the lessons he had learned would be set in motion as his everyday life as an army communicator began. He worked hard to increase his understanding of the terribly complex field. Often the senior sergeants would take him aside and provide individualized lessons to improve his knowledge of complex technical detail. They seemed willing to spend the time since the student was so willing to learn. With every passing day his skills increased. Jim was like a sponge, trying to soak up all he came in contact with.

Keeping his promise to First Sergeant Franklin, Jim enrolled in college level night classes at the army education center, focusing on a degree in business administration. After his duty day was complete, Jim attended scheduled classes, then became a regular sight at the base library where he continued to read and research the subjects he was studying in school.*I did not apply myself in high school,* Jim thought. *I will not make that mistake again.*

Because Ft. Meade was only three hours from home, Jim managed to see Ann almost every week end when he was either not on duty or working on his college lessons. Jim had dedicated the weekdays to work and study, but the weekends were devoted to Ann Carver. Their relationship grew and eventually, planning for marriage became more and more serious. Finally, on the event of his first promotion, Jim and Ann were married. Ann remained at home with her mother and father and Jim came home as often as he could. It was not long before Ann became pregnant with their first child. As if on cue, the army decided to send Jim to Germany, but Ann would not be allowed to accompany him because he did not have sufficient rank to allow an accompanied tour.

The two-year tour did not go quickly. Lori Ann was born six months after his departure and Jim would not see his daughter until she was eighteen months old. During his time in Germany, Jim made it a point to concentrate on soldering excellence and learning all he could about the telecommunications field. After duty each day, he was in either in a college classroom at the education center following his commitment to First Sergeant Franklin or researching subject material at the base library.*Someday,* he thought to himself, *I will become a sergeant, a non-commissioned officer, and when I do, everyone will know I am one of the very best."*

Jim's thoughts often went back to the brief conversation with First Sergeant Franklin and the commitment he had made. But every day that passed convinced him, even more, that he was on the right track.

First Sergeant Franklin was right, Jim often thought. *Every officer I have met has at least a bachelor's degree. They are intelligent and resourceful. I suppose that all comes with the formal education. On the other hand, I see the sergeants around me who lack formal education struggling to be effective. I must make sure that does not happen to me. When I become a sergeant, I will have the formal education to back it up.*

It was a difficult and busy two years, but eventually it ended and Jim returned to the states and a new assignment at Ft. Lee, Virginia. For the first time Jim, Ann, and Lori lived together as a real family. But two years of separation had not been kind. Ann and Jim had matured dramatically during their separation and the once common interests shared in almost everything, had changed.

While Jim's focus was on education and the intellectual side of life, Ann seemed to be lost. She was not sure what she wanted but her thoughts did not match those of her husband.

Time passed quickly as the two of them worked very hard at learning to live together and understanding each other's interests. Eighteen months into the assignment, their second child Allen was born and life for the two young parents focused on caring for and raising their two small children. Life for the small family was good.

Reassignment to Korea came much too soon for the small family. Jim knew his next assignment would be in the far-east, but he had hoped for a two- or three-year tour in the States. After moving his family to St. Louis, Missouri, where Ann's mother and father were stationed with the U.S. Air Force, Jim left for Korea.

This assignment, however, was going to be different from all the others. This was not a training assignment or a job working routine communications systems.

This was an environment where war was expected to break out almost any day and Jim's job was to make sure the communications systems under his management were operating at peak efficiency, twenty-four hours a day. Jim was assigned to a mountain-top communications station on the southern-most tip of South Korea. On a clear day, he could see the coast of Japan in the distance. His job entailed insuring U.S. military communications systems connecting Korea and Japan were in constant readiness to support allied war-fighting forces within Korea should the conflict break out. Jim understood, this was serious business in a place where peace could turn to all-out war at the drop of a hat. He was quickly promoted to Sergeant and placed in charge of all communications operations in the area. *Now*, Jim thought, *Is the time for all that training and education to work it's magic.* After all the years to preparation, Jim had achieved one of his goals – he was now a junior sergeant. It was time to prove to the world that he was not only ready, but more than capable of performing the leadership role.

The high point of Jim's assignment came one bright summer morning with a radio call. His mountain-top communications facility had a helicopter landing pad for emergencies. As Jim sat at his desk preparing one of many operations status reports required by the higher echelons, the air-to-ground radio receiver next to his desk came to life with a call

"Chang-San, this is

Whiskey-Charlie-One, over."

Jim picked up the microphone and responded, "This is Chang-San control, go ahead Whiskey- Charlie-One, over."

The radio crackled, "Roger Chang-San, request permission to land on your site, over."

Jim immediately became suspicious. Only emergency chopper flights landed here and there was no emergency in progress.

Jim keyed the microphone, "Whiskey-Charlie-One, identify yourself, your mission, and purpose for landing, over."

The radio again responded, "Roger Chang-San, we are on a routine United Nations observation mission, we have flown over your site a number of times and we would like to stop for lunch and a visit of your facility. We have a senior U.S. Military Officer on board, over"

Jim had already opened his listing of Allied flights, call signs, missions, and scheduled flights published by U.N. headquarters in Seoul. His book told him Whiskey-Charlie-One was the call sign for an American general officer.

"Whiskey-Charlie-One, permission to land granted. Take landing direction from crew on the ground. See you there. This is Chang-San out," Jim smiled to himself as he reached for the alert phone on his desk.

Jim pressed the mike and spoke slowly, "Security to the helipad on the double. Verify identity of all aboard arriving helicopter. If identity is questionable, take all into custody and hold them pending my arrival."

Jim grabbed his hat and a portable radio set, strapped on a .45-caliber sidearm, then ran out of the building toward the helipad.

As he ran past a Korean technician on duty, he ordered, "Find out where that chopper is from, who is supposed to be on board, and let me know NOW!"

As he approached the helipad, Jim saw the helicopter crew surrounded by a team of armed security soldiers. Each member of the crew was holding their identification cards in front of them while a security guard checked each one.

The portable radio in Jim's hand came to life, "Whiskey-Charlie-One piloted by two U.S. officers, Captains Kelly and Mosby, a senior British NCO, Sergeant Major Gilland, and an

American general, Major General Thompson are passengers. Chopper reported landing for lunch with soldiers at Chang-San Communications Facility."

Jim pulled the mike close to his mouth and answered, "Roger that, thanks."

As he approached the helipad, a tall British Sergeant Major stepped forward and held out his hand to Jim.

"Thanks, you for the invitation to lunch, laddie," he quipped. "We heard you have a very good dining facility here."

"Sergeant Major Gilland, welcome to our site. We are delighted you could stop for a visit," Jim smiled.

The Sergeant Major was a bit surprised when Jim called him by name. "Aye, laddie, my reputation precedes me, does it?' he joked.

"It does, Sergeant Major," Jim responded, "and we are honored by your presence. Welcome to Chang-San," Jim replied.

"Allow me to introduce our commander," the Sergeant Major said as a distinguished looking American Major General arrived at his side. "This is Major General Thompson," he said as he stepped back.

Jim saluted the General and was a bit surprised when the General offered his hand in lieu of a return salute.

"Great job Sergeant. I would have done the same thing if an unidentified chopper tried to land on my site. It's been a long time since I looked down the muzzle of an automatic rifle," he said with a grin on his face.

"Excuse the hostile reception committee, sir," Jim replied. "Since we did not have you on our operations schedule for the day, thought we had better be safe than sorry."

"You bet and I would have expected nothing less than that," the general replied "Anything good for lunch?" he asked.

"Our lifestyle here is modest, sir, but you are more than welcome to join us," Jim replied as he motioned for the General to walk toward the site dining facility.

While the food on this site was always top notch thanks to a very talented Mess Sergeant, lunch on this day turned out to be special. Sirloin steak, baked potato, vegetables, and a salad with bread pudding for dessert. After lunch, Jim brought in his reserve bottle of cognac and everyone enjoyed a toast to the Allied forces stationed in Korea. Then, Jim took the General and his Sergeant Major on a tour of the communications station; the General spent several hours talking to Allied soldiers assigned to the site. All things considered, it was an extremely pleasant day for all.

Finally, General Thompson looked at his watch and said, "Time for us to go."

Jim walked him back to the helipad.

When they reached the aircraft, General Thompson turned around and smiled at Jim. "Sergeant," he began "you have a top-notch operation here. Your security is the best I have seen and morale of your troops is very high. The soldiers here speak highly of you – well done! Thanks to you and your team for a wonderful afternoon."

Jim saluted the senior officer, replying, "Thank you sir, have a good trip home and come back to see us soon."

General Thompson returned the salute, turned on his heel, and boarded the aircraft. Jim watched as the helicopter lifted off and disappeared over the mountains.

The remainder of Jim's tour in Korea was business as usual, until three months before his scheduled departure date.

The phone on his desk rang just at a time when any break from the paperwork was welcome.

The voice at the other end introduced himself as Sergeant Johnson, U.S. Army Assignments Branch, Washington, D.C.

"Your record has come across my desk indicating you are eligible for reassignment," he said firmly. "We have received a by-name request for you to be assigned to a research and development team being pulled together here in Washington with a mission to develop and implement a control subsystem for the new defense department communications satellite program," he concluded.

"Are you interested?" he asked.

"Interested?" Jim questioned. "Never thought I would have a choice. Yes, I would be delighted to get involved with the new satellite program. By the way, where did the by-name request come from?" Jim asked not really expecting an answer.

It came from the Commander, U.S. Army Communications Command, Lieutenant General Thompson. He sent quite a letter to your file. Seems he was very impressed with you earlier this year," Sgt. Johnson explained.

"Hmm," Jim quipped "He got his third star, did not know he was a communications officer, but yes, I met him briefly a few months ago."

"Yes, and as I read this letter, I would guess whatever the occasion, he was very impressed with you," came the reply. "You might be interested to know," Sgt. Johnson continued, "We do not normally assign a junior Sergeant like you to a project as important as this one, but General Thompson is very insistent. He specifically directed that the choice be yours. On the other hand,

I can tell you your record is impressive. Your performance reports are top-notch and the amount of college credit you have earned since arrival on active duty is unusual. I assume you are working toward a degree?" he asked.

"Thanks," Jim replied. "Yes, right now I am working toward a degree in business, but would like to later get into a chemistry program - that will take a while to complete. Yes, I am delighted to accept the assignment and hope someday I will see General Thompson again to thank him for the recommendation," Jim responded.

"Consider it done and if the scuttle-butt I hear is correct, you will see General Thompson again a lot sooner than you might expect. Word is he intends to stay very close to this R and D team as this project is very near and dear to his heart. Have a good trip home and if you have a chance, stop by my office here in Alexandria. I would like to talk to you about the rest of your career," Sgt. Johnson offered.

"Thanks," Jim replied, "I will do that. See you in a few months and thanks again."

Jim laid the phone in its cradle, leaned back in his chair, and started thinking about his tour in Washington, D.C. *Three years in a staff position will leave me plenty of time for night school. Who knows, might even get to know my family again*, he thought wishfully.

After some quick research, Jim learned the agency he would be assigned to was located just across the Virginia state line, on the southern border of Washington, D.C, very close to Ft. Meyer, Virginia. *Past faculty advisors have urged me to choose a home university where I can transfer all my credits to,* Jim reasoned, *Since George Mason University is only a few miles away, I think it wise to talk to them about my degree program. Looks like nothing but good can come from this assignment.*

Chapter VI

Jim thought the flight from Korea to Washington would never end. Ann and the kids had moved from St. Louis to Alexandria, Virginia the month before Jim arrived. Ann found an apartment near a good school and not very far from the agency where Jim would be working.

Homecoming was a great day. Ann and the kids were at Dulles Airport when his flight landed. After almost fourteen months, they were a family once more. Everyone was happy for the first time in a long time as the family settled down for a long, comfortable tour of duty in the nation's capital.

Unfortunately, the fairy tale soon ended. Jim and Ann quickly learned that each of them had continued to mature and change in different directions during their long fourteen-month separation. Their interests had drifted even farther apart than before. It was not long before the disagreements turned to arguments and the frequency became much too often. Both Jim and Ann tried to resolve the ever-expanding gulf between them, but there was little progress. After a while, both learned to hide their problems from the children, but the veil of unhappiness became tighter with every passing day.

Jim was assigned to a large defense agency in Arlington, Virginia specializing in communications services to Department of Defense activities. The research and development team was placed under the guiding hand of Major Donald Tillman and his Senior NCO, Master Sergeant Charles Vinson. Jim had served with both of them before and knew them to be top notch communicators and excellent leaders. Jim was assigned to a research and development team charged with the responsibility of developing a usage and transition process for the multi-satellite system. Jim found the work to be both interesting and challenging. The skills he had developed in his military work, as well as those learned in off duty college studies, seemed to blend into a well-orchestrated algorithm allowing him to identify and solve complex technical problems easily. His reputation grew with every passing day as his interests in his work deepened.

On the anniversary of his promotion to sergeant, twelve months earlier in Korea, Major Tillman surprised him with a promotion to Staff Sergeant. Jim was overjoyed. With the possible exception of his personal life, everything was working out extremely well. He continued to take evening courses at George Mason University and had been placed on the dean's list with a 3.4 grade point average.

The days and months passed quickly. Ann's father retired and returned to the Northern Virginia area to work as a contractor, Ann landed a job at a local department store working in their credit department, and Lori and Allen were in school. Within twelve months, Jim was promoted to Sergeant First Class and placed in a position as a team leader. His personal relationship with Ann continued to deteriorate, but both tried to make the best of a bad situation. There seemed no solution to the problem, so both relaxed and simply tried to make the best of a bad situation, but their relationship was more like that of friends rather than husband and wife. They both put a lot of effort into making each day a good one with as little arguing as possible. Actually, this informal agreement worked rather well and both Jim and Ann outwardly appeared to be happy most of the time. In the end, time solved the problem. Jim's three-year tour of duty was finished and he received orders for Vietnam. Ann decided to remain in Alexandria so the kids could continue in their school and she could continue her job at the department store.

Jim arrived in Nha Trang, South Vietnam one month later, assigned as Operations Sergeant at a large data relay station. The work in the relay center was routine. The computers did all the work and the soldiers and contractors spent all their time making sure the computers were in good operating condition. The real work started when the Viet

Cong chose their base as a target. This was the time when the computers were on automatic pilot while the soldiers practiced their basic stock and trade – combat soldiers.

The company they were assigned to held a responsibility to establish a perimeter defense and hold that perimeter against any ground activity initiated by the enemy. The main perimeter, manned by First Field Forces, was approximately two hundred yards in front of them, so the real responsibility was to back-up the primary perimeter and handle any situation in which the enemy penetrated the primary defensive perimeter, which happened much, much too often. Apart from that, occasional mortar and rocket attacks kept everyone on their toes because they seemed to come at almost any time during the day and night. These attacks always resulted in very long hours on the perimeter, in fox-holes dug deep into the ground for protection. The job was rounded out with occasional assignments to conduct reconnaissance patrols into the jungle gathering intelligence information on enemy force size, location, and activity. These assignments called for a good understanding and remembrance of the basic lessons of soldering and war-fighting taught during basic training. Every now and then, these routine patrols could turn real nasty in a big hurry, but the good part was that previous training had been more than adequate to prepare each soldier for the unpleasant job. Now, all that was left was to gain a little experience in jungle warfare and learn the habits of a very well trained and determined enemy. The rule was simple: Learn your lessons well or you may never have the opportunity to learn anything else.

Shortly after arrival, Jim's first experience under hostile fire came in the middle of the night. The alert sirens sounded, meaning an attack was in progress. As Jim ran out of the barracks with his automatic rifle in hand, mortars started landing all around him. His training and instincts immediately took over. He quickly assessed the direction and frequency of fire, moved away from it until he was able to reach his position on the perimeter. As a Senior NCO, Jim was in charge of a long section of the perimeter containing about fifteen foxholes with two soldiers assigned to each. He established radio contact with other sectors of the perimeter, directed field of fire for the machine guns, then started moving back and forth between positions to make sure everyone was ready in case a fight broke out. The nigh was long, but passed without serious consequences.

With morning sunrise, the attack stopped and life returned to normal. All too often, this scene repeated over and over during the twelve-month tour of duty. With three months remaining, Jim felt confident he had seen it all. Several times enemy infantry penetrated the outer perimeter and Jim had taken a team to track them down. As always, the training had paid dividends and Jim's team was always the one left standing when the shooting was over. Perhaps the worst moment came early in the assignment when Jim realized he had intentionally ended the life of another human being. But the realities of war quickly eased the pain with a sure and certain knowledge that if it had not been the bad guy, it certainly would have been him or one of the soldiers under his command. The sure knowledge that your actions, or lack or if, could cause another American to lose their life made the act of killing the bad guys a lot easier. After a while, killing other people because it was a necessity became much too easy and far too routine for all the American soldiers.

Jim was reminded of that one night when he took a team to look for two enemy soldiers who had penetrated the primary perimeter. It was not difficult to track them down and after a short exchange of gunfire, one of the enemy was dead and the other was wounded. Jim spoke to the enemy soldier in Vietnamese telling him to get on his knees. The soldier did so and looked directly at Jim in the dim light provided by a handheld flashlight.

"Shall I shoot him?" the soldier standing next to Jim asked

"Not unless we have no other choice," Jim replied, "Our special forces team will want to question him."

Jim looked at the face of a very young Viet Cong agent and saw a young man filled with anger and hatred – the expression on his face was unmistakable.

"Keep your hands on your head, do not move, and we will not harm you," Jim told the young soldier.

"Point your rifle directly at his chest, set the weapon to automatic, and do not fire unless I tell you to, but if I give the command, do not hesitate.," Jim instructed the American soldier at his right hand.

"Roger that, Sarge," came the reply.

Jim pointed the flashlight directly into the enemy soldier's eyes and instructed him to stop moving. As the American soldiers watched in disbelief, the young soldier continued to move his hands behind his head. The pained expression on his face made it clear his wound was serious and extremely painful.

"Nyet, Nyet!" Jim shouted in his best Russian, but the soldier continued to move his hands behind his head.

"Shoot, Now!" Jim commanded.

The quiet of the dark night was interrupted with the rapid staccato of automatic gun fire as the rounds from the rifle tore into the Viet Cong soldier's chest.

"Down everybody, down," Jim commanded and each American dropped to the ground and covered his head.

After a few minutes, Sergeant White broke the silence.

"What the hell was that all about?" he asked with a surprised expression on his face.

Jim walked over to the corpse of the dead Viet Cong soldier and gently turned him over onto his face. There, strapped to the base of his neck, was a Russian made hand-grenade. The strap around the soldier's neck, appearing to be a necklace, firmly held the firing pin release mechanism in place, but out of sight.

"He was trying to get to that grenade," Jim pointed out.

"If he had been successful, he would have taken all of us right along with him on his trip to hell. The fact that he had a gunshot wound to the shoulder slowed him down. I suppose he would rather be dead than captured, especially if he could take us along for the ride."

"How did you know?" another soldier asked."Hmm, time for a bit of show and tell," Jim replied.

"When we first caught him, I noticed the thin strap around his neck. From the front, it is supposed to look like a necklace or string for dog tags, but I knew it was holding either a grenade or a bayonet in place. By the way, Viet Cong agents do not wear dog tags for identification as we do.

When he would not stop moving his hands, I knew he was trying to get to it. I suppose being wounded may have clouded his thought processes a bit and that was why he was having trouble getting his hands into the right position. In any case, his training failed and ours prevailed. Let's get back to the line."

Jim inspected the grenade to make sure the pin was still in place, cut the strap releasing the grenade, then lead the soldiers back to their positions on the perimeter, carrying the corpse of the Viet Cong soldier with them.

With less than two weeks remaining on his tour, Jim thought the Viet Cong had learned of his pending departure because they sent their greeting in the form of mortars or rockets almost every day. *I wonder if they know I got one of their boys?* Jim pondered, *Seems to me those mortars are getting closer to my office building every day.*

Rocket and mortar attacks were routine during the day with ground assaults after darkness.

Recon patrols became more and more common and Jim found himself spending more time in the jungle that he had at any time during the tour. But despite the many encounters and more than one close call, the time to leave finally came.

On the morning of his departure, the Battalion Commander, his Sergeant Major, and Jim's Company Commander presented him with the Bronze Star.

As the Colonel pinned the decoration on his chest he quietly said, "All reports indicate you should have a drawer full of these and many should have a 'V' device for valor, but us signal troops are all too often left out of that grand parade. I hope you will find some comfort in the fact that you never lost a soldier in combat and many of our young troops are so much better prepared for combat because of your leadership. Have a good trip home Sergeant, we will miss you around here."

Jim thanked his commanders for their generosity and their leadership. His trip home was filled with memories, some of which he wished he could get out of his head, but all the pleasant ones made it well worthwhile.

Jim's next assignment was at Fort Monmouth, New Jersey at the army signal school. Because of his rank, he was assigned government quarters. The family's new home was a two-story townhouse with three bedrooms and two baths. Ann and the kids relocated soon as school was out and the family began their lives together once more.

Jim's new job was as the head of an automatic data training course. He found teaching to be both challenging and rewarding; he was a natural at it. But while he was the teacher by day, he was the student at night. His evenings were filled with classes in business law, psychology, chemistry, and biology. The year passed quickly and Jim's life was filled to the brim with the world of education.

For most of the year, however, Jim struggled with his health. *Seems every time the wind blows and the temperature drops below 75 degrees, I am sick with something or the other*, he worried. The medics ran test after test, but everything said he was fine. Finally, after a bout with pneumonia, the medics called him in with good news.

Jim met with an older, experienced doctor whose specialty was internal medicine. The doctor was a Colonel and had spent three tours of duty in Vietnam.

"I went back through your records and found before your tour in Vietnam, your body weight was 175 pounds, but after the tour, your weight ran 125 - 130 pounds. For your six-foot height, that means you are under weight – severely underweight!" he proclaimed.

"I know the food in Vietnam was not that great and I have seen a number of cases where our military personnel came back on the verge of malnutrition. I think you fall into that category. I suspect your immune system is nearly out of gas and simply can't fight off even the simplest problem. I would suggest you quit smoking cigarettes, start eating everything in sight, and get your weight back up to 175 or so," the kind old doctor explained.

"Hmmm," Jim replied, "You may be right sir. I long suspected our Mess Sergeant was selling American food on the black market, but we never could pin anything on him. Frankly, the food in our mess hall was worse than most.," Jim explained.

"I was not exactly the first in line at every meal," Jim joked.

"Give it a try," the Colonel said, shaking his finger at Jim "I think you might find yourself getting better real fast."

The diagnosis and prescription were like a minor miracle. Jim quit smoking and, just as the doctor had predicted, his appetite knew no bounds. He could not seem to get enough to eat. In a very short period his weight soared to 180 pounds and he felt like a new person. He combined a rigorous program of daily exercise with a healthy diet and before he knew it, was running two miles a day with little effort; he felt better than any time since army basic training.

"Much more of this," Jim quipped, "And the army will put me on their weight control program."

Jim stopped by the base clinic that week and thanked the doctor for his advice. "I learned an important lesson," he told the Colonel, "I won't let this happen again."

"Good for you Sergeant," the Colonel replied. "I'm glad the cure was a simple one."

From that day forward, Jim felt good all the time. He had to buy a new wardrobe of uniforms, but in the end, his six-foot frame still looked slim and trim. Now, he had more energy than he ever imagined. Those long days and evenings in the classroom were not nearly as tiring and, on many occasions, he would pull a double shift, teaching all day, then substituting on the evening shift for other instructors. He had learned the value of good health and its link to good nutrition and exercise.

But, once again, the end of the good times came quickly. When the phone rang on his desk early one morning, the voice at the other end was more than familiar.

"Hey Arthur Murray, how are the dancing lessons going?" chimed a strong voice from the past.

Jim struggled with a faint memory that would not quite come into focus. Once again, the distant voice broke the silence.

"If it is any consolation, I finally did learn to dance with a girl," he announced. "I liked it so much, I married her."

With that, all the missing pieces of the puzzle fell into place!

"Trevor, where the hell are you and what are you doing?" Jim squealed with delight.

"Took you long enough, Bubba," Trevor replied.

"Yep it is me! To answer your question, I am in Washington, I am still in the army, I work in the army personnel center in Alexandria, and to put a little icing on the cake, I am your career manager!" Trevor proudly replied.

The conversation between two old friends filled a gap in time created by years of separation.

Finally, Trevor brought the conversation to the business at hand.

"I hate to tell you this but, your just came up for reassignment and the destination is back to Vietnam. Yes, yes, I know you just came back last year, but things are heating up over there and we need every experienced NCO we have. I wish I could hold off on this, but I can't." Trevor seemed almost apologetic.

"There is good news, however," Trevor reported.

"You are going to be promoted to Master Sergeant next month, so I want to send you over as a First Sergeant. Funny as it seems, the top sergeant of your old company in Nha Trang is leaving next month. Want his job?" Trevor asked.

Jim thought a moment and replied, "It would appear I have few choices, so I will accept your less than generous offer". Jim laughed.

Trevor chuckled and said, "Okay, and I have one more bit of good news for you. That defense agency you worked for has asked us to send you back to them for another tour. They have a control supervisor job opening up next year in their Hawaii field office and they asked for you to fill it. I will get your orders out for Nha Trang, and from there you will go to Hawaii for a three-year stabilized tour. That sound good to you?" Trevor asked.

Jim smiled from ear to ear. "Yes, old friend," he replied, "And when do, I get to buy you a beer for taking such good care of me."

Trevor's response was quick, "I just came home after three years in Vietnam, I will be here for quite a while. I suppose you will relocate Ann and the kids to Alexandria. When you get here, give me a call before you jump on the big bird for Nha Trang," Trevor responded.

"Will do and looking forward to seeing you soon," Jim said as he placed the phone on the cradle.

Jim's return to his old company was almost like a coming home party. Many of the soldiers there in his first tour had extended and were still there. Jim's commander was a young officer named Captain Jim Carolla. This officer was one of those rare people you meet once in a lifetime who has success written all over him. He held a degree in electrical engineering from Ohio State University and a master's in electrical engineering from UCLA. He was smart, decisive, and not afraid to take a chance when there was no better choice.

"Your friends tell me we are a lot alike," he told Jim on the first day. "I am told you take a somewhat creative approach to problem solving," he said as he patted Jim on the shoulder.

"I have heard that," Jim replied. "I would accept the label of creative," Jim said with a grin.

"Okay," Captain Carolla said, "Suppose we get started. We have a bunch of problems in this company. I have only been here one week, so I think you and I need to put our heads together and get down to business. You probably know this company better than anyone since you spent a year here. I can tell you, not much has changed in the twelve` months you have been gone, except possibly the food in our mess hall has gotten even worse."

Jim smiled at his new commander saying, "I am truly sorry to hear that, sir, but I promise to fix that little problem real soon."

For two days, the new Commander and his First Sergeant stayed behind closed doors mapping out strategy and planning their twelve-month tour in the company. Finally, on the morning of the third day, it was time to start executing their plan.

Jim met Captain Carolla in his office for a short discussion then, suddenly, Jim excused himself and started walking out the room.

"Agenda item, First Sergeant?" Captain Carolla asked.

"Yes sir!" Jim replied. "I've been waiting a long time for this."

Jim walked out of the office and started moving toward the company dining hall. Half way there, the Mess Sergeant, Staff Sergeant Ackerman, was standing in the sun. He had been there on

Jim's first tour and they knew each other really well.

Sergeant Ackerman held out his hand to greet Jim saying, "Welcome back First Sergeant. I hope our little disagreements from your first tour will not cause us any problems?" He said with a sly smile on his face.

It was all Jim could do to hold his anger in check. Jim reached out, took a firm grip on his hand, and pulled him close until they were standing nose to nose.

Jim leaned over Sergeant Ackerman's shoulder and whispered in his ear so that no one else could hear.

"We were not able to catch you during my first tour, but I knew then what you were doing and I know you are still doing it. You may fool everyone in the world by selling American goods on the black market, but this time your little game comes to an end," Jim said firmly with an angry, determined tone in his voice.

Sergeant Ackerman tried to pull back, but Jim held his arm firmly and looked him right in the eyes.

"Do you like western movies, Sergeant?" Jim asked.

Before Sergeant Ackerman could say anything, Jim continued, "If John Wayne were here, he would tell you to pack your personal belongings, get your worthless ass on an aircraft, any aircraft, and be out of this company before the sun sets. If you are here tomorrow when the sun comes up, I promise you, I will personally deal with you very quickly. I would suggest you go to Saigon and tell our battalion Sergeant Major you need a new job, but do not, I repeat, do not show your face in this company ever again after the sun sets on this day. Do you understand me, Sergeant?" Jim said firmly as he pushed Sergeant Ackerman away from him.

Sergeant Ackerman was totally shocked and surprised, but the look on Jim's face told him the game was over. He knew he did not want to call Jim's bluff.

"Very well," Sergeant Ackerman replied. "To Saigon I will go, but you can't prove anything," he responded.

Jim smiled, trying to appear as casual as he could. He looked at the watch on his left arm, then looked up at Sergeant Ackerman saying, "Time's a-wastin', pal. You better get busy. It will be dark before you know it. Last flight to Saigon leaves at 2200."

Jim turned briskly on his heel and walked back to his office.

Captain Carolla was standing at the window of his office and had watched the exchange.

"Well, Top," Captain Carolla said as Jim came through the door "Does this mean we need a new Mess Sergeant?"

"Yes sir, we do," Jim replied with a smile. "That crooked bastard will be out of here before noon, Captain. I talked to the battalion Sergeant Major last night and when Ackerman arrives, he will offer him a choice between terminating his tour and going back to the states with a worse than terrible performance report that will effectively end his army career or a full investigation by the criminal investigation division into his activities of the last two years. I suspect he will run like the coward he is," Jim replied with obvious dislike in his voice.

"Ha," Captain Carolla replied, "I wondered if he would call your bluff. I would like to see what you would have done come tomorrow morning."

"No sir!" Jim quickly replied. "That scene you would want no part of," Jim said seriously as he motioned for the company clerk to come in. "Get First Sergeant Robella at Da Nang Signal Company on the phone," Jim ordered.

"An old friend?" Captain Carolla inquired.

"Yes sir, he is," Jim replied. "He owes me a real big favor and I am going to call it in. He has a young Assistant Mess Sergeant named Bobby Chase working for him. Bobby is the best army Mess Sergeant on the planet – all he needs is a chance to show his stuff. Ted doesn't know it yet, but he will be sending Bobby here on the next aircraft. From now on, Captain, our people are going to eat in one of the finest mess halls in Vietnam."

Captain Carolla, smiled and turned to walk away. As we walked toward his office, he looked over his shoulder and said, "I like your style, Top. we are going to have a good time for the next twelve months."

Sergeant Chase reported to Jim three days later for duty. Jim gave him his marching orders and almost immediately, the company dining facility started changing for the best. In no time at all, fresh fruit and vegetables were the mainstay of every meal. Sgt. Chase announced almost every day to soldiers coming in to eat, "food just like your Mama would make." Within six months, the dining facility was air conditioned and expanded. It looked and functioned like an upscale restaurant back in the states. Everyone in Nha Trang wanted to eat in Sergeant Chase's dining facility.

Jim took full advantage his new dining facility's reputation. He brought in friends from the local special forces group and asked them to redesigned the company's entire defensive perimeter.

New bunkers were built with steel revetment material, new machine guns were brought in and soldiers trained in their use. Motion sensors were positioned at key locations along the perimeter and classes were held to train soldiers in night fighting techniques, hand-to-hand combat, and reconnaissance patrol techniques used in a tropical jungle environment. The soldiers in Jim's company were ready for any fight the well trained, determined Viet Cong enemy might try to dish-out.

In return, the special forces personnel were invited to eat in the company mess hall. Jim thought that was more than a fair exchange. He told his friend who was First Sergeant of the special forces detachment, "I'll keep you and your soldiers well fed, you keep us well trained and equipped." No one ever questioned the relationship.

As the eighth month began, Captain Carolla and Jim were called to Saigon for a meeting with some very special people. A national security organization wanted to establish a very sophisticated telecommunications listening post in Nha Trang to intercept enemy radio signals and pass the intelligence gained from the broadcasts to the appropriate organizations for translation and interpretation. Jim's company had been chosen to provide administrative as well as technical support to the civilian contractors operating the site.

The senior manager of the site was from Dallas, Texas and spoke with an unmistakable, heavy Texas accent. Ned was an accomplished communicator and, like most Texans Jim knew, very friendly. Over the next few months Jim and Ned worked closely as the site was built and tested.

"We just listen," Ned said more than once, "We rarely broadcast and probably would not answer if someone called us on our call sign, which, by the way, is highly classified."

"Hmm," Jim had remarked, "All action and no talk, that seems refreshing."

But over time, as the team from Jim's company worked with Ned and his team of civilians, Jim came to know the operating frequency of that closely guarded call sign. He noted that Ned routinely used one specific radio receiver/transmitter which was set to that specific frequency.

"My favorite radio," Ned often said. "It may be a bit old, but it is a goodie."

Other radio sets in the station were tuned to receive signals from the northern-most reaches of the Vietnam jungle.

Ned's team also monitored U. S. military transmissions as part of his intelligence gathering assignment.

As time passed, American forces in Vietnam were drawing down and the enemy seemed to sense it was time for them to take it easy for a while. Patrols into the jungle and attacks on the base dropped off dramatically, the war seemed so far away for a very short while. But the short rest came to an end when Jim received a call early one morning asking for help.

The special forces group had identified a large enemy force moving what appeared to be rocket launchers and small artillery pieces up the side of a nearby mountain. They asked Jim to send a reconnaissance patrol to find out what was going on. Because of the importance of the mission, Jim decided to head the patrol himself and selected four other jungle patrol experienced soldiers from the company to accompany him. In addition, he appointed his old friend, Sergeant Bob Green to be the radio man. Jim and Bob had been through a large number of jungle patrols in the past and they knew what the other was thinking without asking.

The small patrol entered the dense jungle at mid-morning and made its way to the base of the Bong Do Mountains. About a mile or so ahead, they spotted a large concentration of Viet Cong soldiers on the side of the mountain carefully placing rocket launchers and assembling artillery pieces, all aimed directly at their base. Clearly, a major attack was in the making. Jim pulled his team together and gave detailed instruction to each individual.

"Count and identify the weapons, write down their coordinates, and note anything else needed to pinpoint each exact location," Jim ordered. He instructed Bob Green to turn his receiver off and maintain radio silence until further notice. Members of the team carefully and efficiently went about the dangerous tasks assigned to them.

Just as all needed data was collected and the team was ready to withdraw, all hell broke loose! Jim's team was hit from all sides. It was clear they were surrounded and the enemy did not intend to let any of them get away. Bob Green went down face first as a hand-grenade exploded close behind him. Jim ordered all soldiers to return fire as he checked to see how badly Bob was hit.

"I'm okay, I'm okay!" Bob said as Jim rolled him over. "I think the radio strapped to my back took the hit," Bob whispered.

"Test the radio," Jim ordered, hoping it was not totally destroyed.

Bob turned knobs, changed dial settings and reported with a smile, "Badly damaged, but still working on some frequencies, all our operational frequencies with special forces are out of commission."

Jim's mind was racing as small arms fire from the enemy intensified. He pulled his note pad out, wrote a frequency on it and handed it to Bob.

"Tune to this frequency," Jim commanded.

Bob looked at the number and shook his head, "Can't do that boss, that is not an authorized frequency. In fact, I think use of that frequency is prohibited because its user is highly classified."

"Just do it, that's an order Sergeant," Jim commanded. "Hand me the mike when you are ready."

Bob set the radio and handed the mike to Jim

"Your dime boss," Bob said.

"Thanks," Jim replied. "This may be illegal as hell, but jail will look good compared to what they have in store for us" Jim said pointing toward the advancing enemy forces.

Jim keyed the mike and calmly spoke, "CQ, CQ, this is Nha Trang Recon, Come in, over."

Jim released the transmit key on the side of the mike and waited.

The receiver was silent.

Jim keyed the transmitter again saying, "CQ, CQ, this is Nha Trang Recon. This is the First Sergeant, we are surrounded by enemy forces and will be overrun in a matter of minutes. We need help! Come in, over."

After what seemed a life-time, a voice with a distinct Texas accent, replied, "Tell me what you need Nha Trang Recon."

Jim replied, "We are surrounded and under intense fire." Jim gave the map coordinates of their position.

"We need air support and lots of it" Jim continued.

"Stand-by," came the reply.

Again, a life time passed, but then a different voice came over the radio saying, "Nha Trang Recon, this is Silver Angel. I am right on top of you and I brought the whole farm with me.

Where do you want it? Over."

Jim keyed the mike, "You have our coordinates, give us fifty yards and surround us with it, over."

"Get your heads down boys, here it comes," was the reply.

Suddenly, the jungle erupted into one huge fireball. Flames, smoke, and explosions were on all sides. The ground shook as the explosions intensified. Trees, debris, and dirt filled the air as the team huddled as close to the ground as they could. Jim knew the ordnance was close, very close, because he could feel the heat from the flames. Bits of shrapnel filled the air. Intense explosion after explosion lasted for what seemed a lifetime. Heavy ordnance and napalm turned the jungle into a burning hell-on-earth as the jet aircraft made pass after pass in their coordinated attack.

Then, suddenly as it started, all was quiet.

The receiver on the radio came to life again saying, "Keep your heads down boys, we got most of it but we have asked our army chopper friends right behind us to come in and clean things up. Glad we could help; this is Silver Angel out."

Jim heard the roar of jet engines as the fighters made one final, low-level pass over their position. Jim looked up in time to see three air force jet aircraft bank sharply and fly away.

Another voice boomed over the radio, "Stay where you are Nha Trang Recon, we see you and need to take care of a few of your friends who are wondering around. Let's get 'em, boys."

Multiple machine guns came alive with a sound that was music to Jim's ears. Slugs from the helicopter mounted machine guns hit the jungle foliage and floor with loud thuds just yards from their position. Systematic death rained down from on high for the longest time. Some of the hits were so close, jungle debris loosened by the slugs flew through the air around members of the recon patrol. After a while, the shooting stopped and the radio came to life again.

"Ok Nha Trang Recon, that about does it, we have a chopper setting down 100 yards south of your position, the express bus for Nha Trang departs in five minutes – all aboard!" the radio went silent.

The flight back to base was a quiet one. No one hurt, no one wounded or injured, everyone scared as hell.*I'm not even thirty yet, but I am getting much too old for this kind of stuff,* Jim thought as the chopper set down on the base helipad.

Captain Corolla met the team with a smile.

"Heard you stirred up quite a party out there," he quipped.

"I'm told the other guys did not have any fun at all!" he joked as he came along side Jim.

He put his hand on Jim shoulder affectionately and said quietly "You and the team okay, Top?"

"Yes sir," Jim replied, "Just tired as hell, but compared to our friends out there on the side of the mountain, we are just fine."

As Jim and the recon team walked back to their company area, Jim told his team, "Guys, I would rather be lucky than good any day and this was one of those very lucky days we will live to tell our grandchildren about."

Bob Green turned around laughing, "You want to tell us who you made that radio call to?"

"I'm not sure I should do that. Let's just say on this day, I had a guardian angel in my corner that the Viet Cong did not know about and he has one hell of a Texas accent," Jim offered.

"If you see him again, will you tell him I love him and ask him to marry me?" Bob asked.

"You're already married," Jim laughed. "But I'll be sure to give him the message and if I get to see your wife Betty, I will tell her as well."

The next day, Jim drove to the listening site expecting to thank his Texas friend, but when he pulled up in front of the building, a sign on the door made it clear, the message would not be delivered. The handwritten sign read, "Gone back to Texas. Welcome home Nha Trang Recon."*Ned knew I would come here. This message is for me,* Jim thought to himself. *Ned compromised his location to save our skin, but had to leave as a result of it. I suppose I will never be able to say thanks to his face.*

Jim climbed back into his jeep, but as he pulled pass the door where the sign hung, Jim said aloud "Thanks Ned. I hope someone returns the favor to you someday."

Jim drove back to the company where he quietly completed his tour of duty. At the end of twelve months, Jim's second tour of duty in Vietnam came to an end as a complete success.

He earned two Bronze Stars and a number of lesser decorations, but all he wanted was for the soldiers under his control to do what had to be done during their tour of duty, then return to their

families safe and sound. At the end of his tour, not one soldier in his company died in combat.

Jim was proud of that record. He was also eternally grateful to a friend from Texas, a friend he would not see again, but one he would never forget.

Chapter VII

The three-year tour in Hawaii was great. After a tough year in Vietnam, the rest was more than welcomed. Jim, Ann, Lori, and Allen were a family once again. The weather was better than great - warm all year - the scenery was remarkable, and the family lived comfortably in government provided quarters on Schofield Barracks. Compared to the pressures of his year in Vietnam, this assignment was more like a paid vacation.

Unfortunately, the division between Jim and Ann had grown even worse and nothing seemed to bridge the gap. Both of them tried and tried, but there was too much water under the bridge; the relationship was lost and both partners knew it.

As it has so many times in the past, fate intervened, but this time her hand was gentle.

"Do you feel like a ping-pong ball?" Trevor asked.

"I'm not sure what you mean by that," Jim replied. "But I am happy as hell that you are still my career manager."

"In your case, there is no management to it. The agency has requested that you be selected to head a new program back at their Washington headquarters," Trevor explained. "I can give you that or send you to Ft. Gordon to take the first sergeant job in one of the signal school companies, your choice."

"Pal," Jim began, "I don't have to think about that one for long. I really do need to be back in Virginia for a while. I have some personal business to take care of."

"Virginia it is," Trevor replied. "Perhaps this time we can have more than one beer together?"

"If I could, I would buy you the brewery," Jim quipped. "See you soon and thanks one more time."

When Jim gave the news to Ann, she summoned the courage to discuss the subject both of them had avoided for so long.

"Just take me and the kids back to Alexandria, buy us a house, get us settled in, and then it will be time for you to go," Ann said with a pained look on her face.

Jim knew she was right. He had searched his mind and conscience time and time again for a solution, but could not find an answer.

"Okay, okay," he replied. "But at least you and I need to be close friends, for the children's sake. If they feel we are close, but just can't live together, it will make it easier for them to accept," Jim reasoned.

"I agree," Ann said. "We will probably make better friends and get along better than we ever did as husband and wife."

Jim thought he detected a brief smile on her lips as the tension between the two of them eased for the first time in a long while.

"You do understand that we will have to live together for a while in your new house, but I promise to make it as easy on you as I can," Jim offered.

"Yes," Ann replied, "and I will do the same."

For the first time in many, many years, their relationship was warm and forgiving. It seemed a tremendous weight had been removed from their shoulders. The remaining months of the tour in Hawaii passed uneventfully.

In the spring, the family returned to Virginia and bought a comfortable home in Woodbridge. Ann found a good job with the government, the kids were enrolled in school, and Jim prepared to begin a new tour of duty with the agency. He immediately enrolled in night school at George Mason University and started taking classes he hoped would eventually lead to a degree. As soon as Ann was settled in her new job, Jim moved into a small apartment near the office. They went to an

attorney and completed paperwork to establish a formal separation, but Jim did not want a divorce until his military career was over, so they both agreed to wait. In the meantime, each was free to carry on their personal life, to include dating, but neither Jim nor Ann were in the mood for that.

Jim reported for duty at the agency and found himself facing Lt. Colonel Scarsdale on the first day. He was a relatively young Air Force officer with over twenty years' service. Jim felt very comfortable with him.

"Colonel Henderson is on temporary duty in Europe and his admin assistant, Carolyn Hecht, is on vacation," he patiently explained.

"As you can see, your new office is being remodeled and should be ready shortly. In the meantime, I will place you in the office with Sergeant Dickerson. For the next couple weeks, until Colonel Henderson and Carolyn return, reacquaint yourself with the agency. I know you still have a great many friends here and I would guess many of them will be most helpful in your new job," he explained.

"I don't want to attempt a detailed explanation of your duties, I think Col. Henderson would want to do that, but I am sure you already know most of it. We need to do a better job managing our enlisted personnel, so until the good colonel returns, give that some thought and start any initial groundwork you feel necessary. If I can help, feel free to drop in. One thing I will tell you, however, is that the army was very reluctant to give you a back-to-back joint service tour after Hawaii, but apparently Lieutenant General Thompson, our former director, had some say in the decision and here you are." Lt Col Scarsdale stood up and offered his hand.

Jim thanked him for his time and the very generous offer, turned, and walked to Sergeant Dickerson's office.

Jim stuck his head in the door of Sergeant Dickerson's office saying, "I understand I am to be your guest for a short time."

Sergeant Dickerson looked up, rose to his feet, and met Jim at the door.

"Tom Dickerson," he said, offering his hand. "My friends call me Dickie." He smiled.

Jim took his hand. "Thanks for giving me a place to call home," he replied. "I am Jim and happy to meet you."

A second desk had been moved into the large office, so Jim settled into the comfortable chair and began to unpack his brief case. As he looked out the door, he noticed a large office with a name plate of Carolyn Hecht over the door. At the desk was a very short, very plump girl talking on the phone. As she turned around in her chair, Jim noted she was wearing a very short mini-skirt. When she stood up, he quickly concluded she did not have the legs or the figure for a dress so short.

"Oh well, for two weeks or so, I can handle the view," he mumbled to himself as he looked away. "Perhaps my new office will be ready ahead of schedule."

The next two weeks went by quickly. On Friday evening as he departed, Lt. Colonel Scarsdale stopped by to tell him the new office would be ready by Tuesday or Wednesday of the next week and Jim could move in at his leisure.*Perhaps I will find a way to tell Sara, the short, plump, temporary secretary all about the benefits of ladies' slacks*, Jim thought to himself.

The weekend passed quickly. Bright and early on Monday morning, Jim settled at his desk in Dickie's office to read a stack of documents explaining selection procedures for joint-service enlisted personnel for duty at the agency. After reading for quite a while, he looked up just in time to see a tall, slender, lady dressed in a short pink skirt walk into the office. Her short, auburn brown hair framed a doll-like face of delicate, soft features. A set of round brown eyes added a soft quality of beauty that seemed to pull your attention from the rest of her all too perfect figure. All the curves were in the right places and her long, slender legs gave every movement of her body the appearance of grace in motion.

Jim almost choked on the mouthful of coffee he was trying to swallow.

"That," he said emphatically, "is more like it" as he watched the, tall, beautiful lady slowly settled into a chair at the desk and cross her long, shapely legs.

"I need to check my pulse to see if my heart is still beating," Jim said aloud.

The lady was stunning! Jim could not believe how pretty she was and how tastefully she was dressed. She looked up, but apparently could not see that she was being watched, carefully watched. She turned her back to the door and began shuffling papers on her desk.

"Did you say something?" Dickie asked.

"Is that Carolyn Hecht, Colonel Henderson's admin assistant?" Jim asked pointing at the lady in pink.

"Yep, that's her. Just back from a two-week vacation," Dickie responded.

"We quietly refer to her as the Iron Lady, behind her back, of course. She is Colonel Henderson's right and left hand. She runs this division with an iron hand and makes everyone think Colonel Henderson is doing the job. Everyone in the division likes her a lot," Dickie said, waving his hands in front of him. "Not only is she pretty as hell, but she is really good at what she does," he commented with an admiring look on his face.

"Would you like an introduction?" Dickie asked.

"No, thank you, I think I can handle that job all by myself," Jim confidently replied.

Jim sprang from his chair and quickly covered the short distance to the door of Carolyn Hecht's office.

He knocked on the door frame gently and when she turned and looked at him, he gave her his best boyish smile, saying "Could it be you are Mrs. Hecht?"

Carolyn rose to her feet, extended her hand with a smile, saying, "Carolyn, call me Carolyn."

Jim took her warm hand in his trying to display his best smile again, but his brain had turned to mush – he was speechless.

Before he could offer a single word, Carolyn opened her lovely mouth saying "And I bet you are Sergeant Jim Knight, I have been expecting you."

Jim didn't want to release her hand, but recovered his senses, found his voice, and released her hand.

"Yes ma'am, everyone calls me Jim. Colonel Henderson told me to look you up as soon as I arrived. He said you would take good care of me?" Jim responded, trying to hide his fascination with the colonel's choice of words.

Carolyn gazed at the tall army Sergeant, neatly dressed in his tailored, green uniform with shoes that looked like glass. His long blonde hair was neatly combed and his emerald green eyes seemed to look directly into her heart.

"I thought all you army types cut their hair very short," she said with a smile growing across her lips.

"Yes ma'am, most of us do, but I prefer to wear mine a little longer than most. I suppose you could say it is just barely within army standards," Jim timidly replied.

Carolyn's heart began to beat a little faster as this tall, handsome soldier gazed at her from a distance much too close for her comfort. She could feel her face flush, but struggled to hide her emotions. This new army sergeant had truly made an impression on her.*I hope he cannot see the effect he is having on me; I need to get myself under control,* Carolyn thought to herself.

"Please, sit down Sergeant," Carolyn said, waving toward a chair at the end of her desk.

"Thank you," Jim replied, "But please, call me Jim, Sergeant seems so formal," he said as he settled into the chair.

Carolyn turned her back to him as she waked around her desk, took a deep breath, then sat down in her chair and crossed her shapely legs. Jim thought his heart was going to stop as he watched. He quickly regained his composure and looked, again, into her smiling face. He was struck by her simple beauty - not much make-up, nothing artificial, just plain, simple natural beauty. Jim had seen a lot of beautiful women in his life, but this one was very special.

Dickie watched from the door of his office with a big smile on his face. *Hmmm*, he thought.

"Perhaps the Iron Maiden has met her match," he said under his breath.

"It does not take a science teacher to see there is more chemistry going on between those two than either of them would like to admit," he chuckled. *I bet the next two or three years are going to be very interesting around here*, he thought as he walked out of his office and down the hall to the cafeteria.

"Yes sir, I bet the Sergeant and the Iron Lady are going to make quite a team around here," he said under his breath as he walked through the door of the cafeteria.

Carolyn and Jim discussed his new job at length.

"This is all new to the agency," she said, "And for that reason, you will be attempting to do things we have never done before; you may encounter some resistance from the hard liners. After all, management of military personnel working here, especially career management, is the responsibility of their parent military department, army, air force, etc. Now, all of a sudden, a major defense agency is suggesting they should become involved in that role. You could end up on the wrong side of your own military department," Carolyn speculated.

Carolyn was a wise lady who had a good understanding of the agency and how it works.

"I suppose," he replied thoughtfully, "The best way to solve the problem would be to first figure out exactly what the problems really are, then make sure the solution is a benefit to not only the individual and our agency, but to each of the military departments as well," he said with a smile.

"I have no doubt you will figure it out and be successful," Carolyn replied. "Colonel Henderson tells me you are very thorough in your work and one who has a unique, imaginative approach to problem solving," she said as she leaned back in her chair.

"Colonel Henderson will be here this afternoon and is anxious to talk to you about your assignment. I will call you soon as he arrives," she said as she rose to her feet.

Jim knew the meeting was over. He rose to his feet, shook her warm hand again, and thanked her for her time. He slowly walked out of the office and down the hall to find an old friend. As he walked the crowded hallway, his thoughts were filled with images of Carolyn. *Beauty and brains, all in one very attractive package*, he thought as he walked. *Unfortunately, that wedding ring on her left hand tells the story, On the other hand, I can't help but wish…*

Carolyn fell into her chair and stared at the wall on the other side of her desk. Her two-week attempt to salvage her marriage had met with total failure. In the end, George had told her he saw no reason to remain married, but the thought of divorce was even worse. Carolyn knew the relationship was over. Now all that remained was the formality of a break up. She knew this was not going to be a happy time for her or the children, but somehow, they would get through it.

Now, all of a sudden, she felt like a teenage high school girl who had just met someone special who filled her every thought.*Get him out of your head*, she thought to herself. *That wedding ring on his left hand means he is spoken for and that is the end of that. From now on, our relationship must be strictly professional and that is the end of it. I have enough problems without having school-girl feeling for a married man*, she thought.

Carolyn felt better after that little talk with herself. *Friends, perhaps, but nothing more. End of story*, she concluded.

The next year went by much too fast. His work at the agency was moving along extremely well, supported not only by the agency staff, but the military departments as well. Almost every day was filled with meetings which included Carolyn. They were constantly together working issues involving not only the enlisted staff, but officers as well. More and more they talked to each other about their personal lives and families. It wasn't long before each of them was disappointed when the day did not include some time together. Finally, during lunch while attending a meeting together at the Pentagon, Jim noticed the wedding ring on Carolyn's left hand had been replaced by a simple ruby birthstone ring.

"A change of fashion?" Jim inquired as he touched the ring on her left hand.

"More like a change in lifestyle," Carolyn commented.

"George and I finally gave up and this past week end I moved into a small apartment with the children. We are getting settled in, but I have no idea how to connect the TV set," she said with a look of dismay on her face.

"Invite me to dinner!" Jim blurted out.

"I will have that TV set humming in a matter of minutes," he said confidently.

"Is there anything else electronic you need connected?" he asked with a big smile on his face.

"Yes," Carolyn replied, "There are actually two TV sets and a couple clock-radios that I can't seem to figure out."

"Great," replied Jim. "I know you don't need another guy stomping around your house just a few days after separating from your husband, so just tell the kids that I am a friend and am willing to help."

"That's wonderful!" Carolyn replied. "How about this Saturday afternoon about four o'clock? I will tell the kids and we will be looking forward to it," she smiled. "

By the way, I know you and Ann are separated, when do you intend to take off the ring?" Carolyn asked.

"Oh," Jim replied staring at his left hand. "Been meaning to do that, just had not gotten around to it yet. I suppose old habits die hard," he replied with a boyish look on his face.

"I didn't mean to pry into your personal life. I suppose I should not have said that," Carolyn said with a look of embarrassment on her face.Jim looked into her eyes and gently placed his hand on hers.

"Not at all," he softly replied, "I intended to take it off long ago, just forgot. There is absolutely no reason to continue wearing it," he said gently.

Carolyn's face brightened. The embarrassed look was replaced with a gentle smile.

"I am looking forward to this Saturday, don't be late," she ordered.

It was the longest week of his life. They worked together most of the week, but nothing more was mentioned of the first date. Jim tried his best to hide his feeling of anticipation, but deep down inside, he was overjoyed. Finally he would see the pretty lady in the pink dress in a personal setting rather than a professional one.

Finally, Saturday arrived. Jim arrived at Carolyn's apartment at four o'clock sharp. He had a small bouquet of flowers for her and a full gallon of ice cream for the kids. He was an instant success!

Within minutes he had both TV sets connected and working. Robin and Mike were happy as they could be. Before dinner was served, both clock-radios were connected and set. As an added chore, Jim installed a number of pictures and prints on the walls of Carolyn's apartment.

Dinner was a great experience.

"How do you like our cheese spaghetti?" Robin asked.

It's wonderful!" Jim replied. "This is the first time I have ever had cheese spaghetti," he announced.

"Wow!" Mike exclaimed. "We have it all the time. Maybe you will come back if we serve it again?"

"Well, thank you," Jim replied. "I would be delighted to accept your most generous invitation," he said as he patted Mike's head.

"Do you play baseball?" Mike asked.

"Yes, I do," Jim replied. "Perhaps we can play together next time I come back," Jim suggested as he looked across the table at Carolyn for approval.

Carolyn nodded saying, "Perhaps we should make that real soon, okay Mike?"

"Oh yes Mom," Mike replied, "Real soon."

"Do you know anything about baby dolls?" Robin asked.

"Yes, I really do," Jim replied. "I have a son and a daughter and my daughter has taught me all about baby dolls," Jim boasted.

"Then you come back really, really soon so we can play baby dolls after you and Mike play baseball," Robin said with a tone of authority.

"Looks like you are a real hit around here," Carolyn offered as she reached out to touch Jim's hand.

Jim looked into Carolyn's eyes and replied, "You cannot know how good this feels."

Carolyn replied saying, "Perhaps I really do."

The next year passed more quickly that either Jim or Carolyn could imagine. Soon Lori and Allen met Robin and Mike and a lifelong friendship started. Carolyn and Jim continued to work together each week day and spent every minute of the week-ends together. Jim met Carolyn's family and was soon accepted into the close family group. After Carolyn met Jim's family; it seemed like the two of them had been together forever.

Colonel Henderson soon retired and was replaced by Colonel Hugo. He was a very relaxed individual, well-liked by everyone in the agency. Jim's relationship with his new boss was a very close one.

Soon after his arrival, Colonel Hugo called Jim and Carolyn into his office, closed the door, and announced, "I have marching orders for both of you, listen closely. Carolyn is being promoted to a position as my Executive Officer. Jim, you are my personal enlisted assistant - much like a First Sergeant. Both of you will be given orders from me to perform special tasks. I have total confidence in both of you, so when the orders come, simply execute as you always do and everybody will be happy. Jim, I will not always be able to talk directly to you, so when Carolyn passes my orders to you, take it as coming directly from me. You two need to get close to each other because while I am here, you will be working very closely, doing very special tasks. Any questions?

"No sir," replied Jim, "I got it."

"I understand sir," replied Carolyn.

"Good," replied Colonel Hugo. "Let's get on with it"

He waved his hand as a sign of dismissal and both Carolyn and Jim walked out of the office together.

As they walked together down the hall, Jim leaned close to Carolyn and said, "We have been given orders to get closer to each other. We must make a point to carry out our orders to the best of our collective ability."

"I understand," Carolyn whispered. "I always follow orders from my boss right to the letter."

Both Jim and Carolyn smiled at each other knowingly as they walked side by side into the cafeteria.

The days turned into weeks, weeks turned into months, and before he knew it another year was gone. Carolyn had bought the house her and George owned when they were married as part of the divorce settlement and moved back in, their divorce made final after a year. Jim moved in with Carolyn and the children while work at the agency became successful beyond Jim and Carolyn's dreams. Carolyn was again promoted as Mr. Simmonds brought her back into the resource management organization as a resource analyst. Everything was falling into place as Jim approached his eighteenth year of active duty. But, as it had many times before, fate intervened. This time, her hand was heavy.

His tour of duty came to an end and the army decided to send him overseas. Jim met with his career manager to ask for a tour extension, but it was not going to happen. Jim was going to Germany for a twenty-four-month tour of duty as first sergeant of a large signal company located in Hanau, Germany.

"Where the hell is Trevor when I need him?" Jim repeated many times over.

Carolyn was visibly shaken by the news. "Seems like every time my life gets on a positive track, everything goes crazy," she commented over and over.

"It is not the end of the world," Jim tried to reassure her.

"We will get through this just like we have everything else. We simply must have faith in each other." Jim told her.

Carolyn was clearly disappointed, but she quickly adjusted and before long her attitude leaned more toward planning for the time when Jim would return from the two-year visit to Germany.

"Perhaps I will come over for a two or three week visit after you have had a chance to settle in. Then you can give me a guided tour of Europe!" Carolyn offered with a gleam in her eye.

"Hmmm," Jim pondered, "As I recall, Europe, and in particular Paris, is a nice place to visit any day of the year, but I like springtime in Europe," Jim explained.

From that day forward, it was never a question of "if" only "when". Planning for a vacation in Europe for Carolyn was now set in concrete and the subject of many follow on conversations between the two of them - the stage was set.

The subject of when to make the relationship permanent came up often. Both Jim and Carolyn agreed that while he was on active duty, marriage was more of a complication to both careers than a benefit. Clearly, Carolyn could not leave the Washington area and, in particular, she did not want to leave the agency because she knew everything was in place, including a strong mentor, to guarantee a successful career. On the other hand, Jim's military career had also been very successful and now he had reached a crossroads where a tough decision was in the making.

"I have a good record," Jim reasoned. "It makes sense to me that this tour in Europe is nothing more than setting the stage for my selection to the Sergeants Major Academy, then another tour somewhere overseas as a command sergeant major. When all is said and done, that means I am looking at thirty to thirty-five years in the army with an eventual retirement as a Sergeant Major. In the long term, the end-result is a monthly retirement income somewhere in the neighborhood of $1,500.00 as opposed to an income of $1,200.00 if I retire as a first sergeant."

Jim knew the ropes as a First Sergeant. "Been there, done that, got the tee shirt to prove it," he argued referring to his tour of duty as a First Sergeant in Vietnam.

"If I can be successful as a First Sergeant in combat, the job in a peace-time environment would be a piece of cake," he argued with himself. "I can do this job in Germany with both hands tied behind my back. The decision," he reasoned, "is do I want one career in the military or should I end that career, finish my education, then start a second career early enough to retire a second time at a reasonably young age.

If I take the thirty-plus years career in the military, I might as well kiss Carolyn and any hope for a family life goodbye, because she cannot relocate to accommodate my career assignments," he reasoned.

"If, on the other hand, I take the second career road option, I have a small retirement income with all the military benefits, I have the chance to not only start over again, but this time, I can have a family, a good education, and perhaps a second career that would allow me to reach for the brass ring," he concluded.

"Tired of being poor, sweetheart?" Carolyn often asked as Jim worked through this line of reasoning.

"I have always wondered what it would be like to have more money than just that needed to live each day," Jim would respond.

"Wouldn't it be nice if we could have a life together where we worried about many things but money was not one of them?" Jim asked.

In the end, the decision was an easy one. Jim would take the assignment to Germany because he had little or no choice. But that would be his last assignment in the army. As soon as his twenty-four-month tour was finished, he would retire, return to Carolyn and the family, get married, and go back to school to finish his degree program. From there, a second career would begin. This choice held a great promise of prosperity for Jim and Carolyn. The decision was made, agreed to, and set in concrete. Both Jim and Carolyn almost looked forward to the twenty-four-month separation as a means to the end they both wanted.

"The twenty-four months won't be all that bad," Jim reasoned. "I will come home every three months for a week or so and you can come over in the next three months for a week or so and we can make the time pass very quickly doing that."

That line of logic made the whole pending experience much easier to take. Both Jim and Carolyn accepted their plan and started planning their future together as a family. On the day of his departure, Carolyn drove him to the airport. As he walked away to board the aircraft, Carolyn waved with tears in her eyes.

"I'll see you in three months, sweetheart," Jim called out as cheerfully as he could.

"Someday, real soon, this will all be over," Carolyn replied affectionately.

Jim smiled and blew her a kiss as he turned to walk away.*It can't be soon enough for me. For the next two years, I am going to be a very lonely puppy!* Jim thought to himself as he entered the aircraft.

Chapter VIII

Jim arrived at his new assignment, the 261st Signal Company, in the early spring of 1977. It had been fifteen years since he was last in Germany, but some of the customs and language began to come back quickly. Jim was taken directly from the Frankfurt airport to battalion headquarters for his entry briefing by the battalion commander and battalion sergeant major. During the discussions, both made it simple and clear. This company had suffered dramatically under a number of poor commanders and first sergeants. When a new commander and first sergeant were requested from Washington, an army lieutenant General Thompson had become involved and ordered two people to take the jobs of cleaning up this company.

"Captain Steve Norman is probably the best young office I know of. He has already had two company commands and each time he was brought in to solve and fix the kinds of problems this company is experiencing. In both cases, he was totally successful. This is a job for Steve, even though I suspect he will not be happy with a third consecutive command position. I bet he is thinking it is time for a soft staff job," General Thompson was quoted as saying.

"As his First Sergeant, I am sending Jim Knight to do the job. I have known Jim for a long time and I know him to be an extremely capable, intelligent, and resourceful NCO. He is the NCO Steve needs to solve this problem once and for all," came General Thompson's final word.

The Battalion Commander, Lt Colonel Martin, made his position very clear to Jim.

"I am told you may be the best choice for this job. In the end, I'll be the judge of that, but make no mistake First Sergeant, make a mess of this and I will fire you so fast your head will swim. Do we understand each other?" he asked in a very firm voice.

"Yes sir," Jim replied. "I understand perfectly "But I can assure you sir, I have not failed at this kind of job in the past and do not intend to start now."

As Jim opened the door to leave the office, Lt. Col. Martin called out, "If you need help First Sergeant, do not hesitate to let me know. I am on your side in this," he said with an almost friendly smile. "Oh, by the way, General Thompson sends his regards, him and I also go back a long way," Lt. Col. Martin said.

"Thank you sir," Jim replied "I may need to take you up on that before this is over."

Jim closed the door and walked into the office of Command Sergeant Major George Lott.

The Sergeant Major gave Jim a two-hour briefing on his perspective of the company. While there were many, many problems, it appeared to Jim that everything was rooted in a total lack of leadership, lack of management experience, and poor organization.

"Everyone in that company is going in two different directions and no-one is getting anywhere," the Sergeant Major concluded.

"Let me be honest with you, Jim," the Sergeant Major said with a stern look on his face, "I know of your reputation for what I'll just call creative problem solving. Yep, I checked you out and I know you take a creative, often unorthodox, approach to dealing with problems. And I also know you have an even greater reputation for bending the rules in the interest of getting a job done. If it is any consolation, your reputation also says you are extremely effective. My sense tells me given a little support, you are more than capable of getting this mess cleaned up, especially with the backing of an excellent commander such as Steve Norman." He smiled as he waved his hands in the air.

"I'm okay with all that," he continued. "I have given this a lot of thought and I strongly suspect this approach is exactly what we need to fix the problem. So, I've got your back, go ahead and do what you need to do and I will cover for you. But I would appreciate it if you would let me know ***before*** Rome starts burning to the ground," he said with an inquiring expression on his face.

"I understand completely, Sergeant Major," Jim replied. "I'll make sure you are the first to hear if Nero starts playing his violin. I appreciate the vote of confidence and thanks, in advance, for the cover. I suspect I will need that more than anything I can think of at the moment. I'll keep you posted."

Jim shook the Sergeant Major's hand and walked out of his office. As he walked down the hall, he heard the Sergeant Major's voice, behind him.

"Oh, by the way, welcome back to Germany First Sergeant."

Jim smiled and continued down the hall. It was time to get to work. This might not be as easy as he had anticipated!

The first three or four months took every moment of Jim's time and every ounce of his energy. The hours were long and the work difficult. Jim organized the NCOs of the company into a management team.

"You are the managers that make this company work. It's time for you to start working together instead of against each other," Jim lectured at his first general meeting.

Jim assigned roles and responsibilities requiring the Sergeants to work closely with each other to reach a common goal, then forced them to deal with problems facing the enlisted personnel of the company. To round out the focus, Jim called in all the dependent wives and husbands, then organized them into a problem-solving team. They established a monthly meeting schedule and conducted their get-togethers as a business meeting complete with an agenda, special working group assignments, and other tasks and responsibilities causing the group to be not only effective in their roles, but enthusiastic in the work as well.

Before long, results were rolling in and the word of the company's success began to spread. There was more than one time when Sergeant Major Lott had to step in to run interference for Jim but in the end, the results more than justified the means. The company began to function efficiently and once the management processes were refined and improved, they began to reach out to other companies and organizations within the military community to offer their assistance and advice. Over a very short timeframe the company's reputation as a source of pro-active assistance quickly spread over the local community as well as others within Germany.

In a later telephone conversation with another Sergeant Major, Sergeant Major Lott admitted, "Yes, yes, I have heard more than once that good results more than justify the means and now I am beginning to become a believer of that gospel, but I will not admit to saying that, especially not to Jim Knight," he confessed. "Yes, Jim had to cut a few corners and pushed a few senior people around a bit in order to get the results he was looking for, but I will tell you the model set by Jim's people is a good one and while I cannot force you to follow his example, I will tell you his group is the talk of the town and the good work he has done serves the best interests of all our enlisted people!"

But Jim knew his trip to success in this assignment had not been without a high degree of risk and difficulty. During his career he had been careful not to make serious mistakes and even more careful not to make enemies. Unfortunately, he had failed in this department. During his tours in Vietnam, he had alienated one NCO to the point that neither wanted anything to do with the other. Unfortunately, this NCO had remained in the army and had been extremely successful. At this point in his career, he was the Command Sergeant Major one echelon above George Lott which made him a part of Jim's chain of command. Sergeant Major Lott had held him at bay and protected Jim from his wrath, but because of his seniority, George Lott was forced to give in on what he called the "small stuff". This all came to a head when the command was scheduling a formal dining-in ceremony to honor the retirement of a General officer in the command.

"I tried to reason with him," Sergeant Major Lott pleaded, "But after all, he is our senior Command Sergeant Major and as such he does have a few prerogatives."

"Just because I am the only single First Sergeant in the command does not give him the right to interfere in my personal life," Jim argued.

"Calm down," George Lott pleaded. "He is only trying to make this function go as smoothly as possible. For that reason, he wants all our First Sergeants to be escorted by their wives. Since you do not have one, he insists on appointing an official escort for you."

"That's fraternization," Jim argued. "Using a female junior NCO, especially one in my own company, as an official escort is not right."

"Your point is well taken, but this time, the discussion is over. SSG Carol Anderson will be your official escort. She should wear a gown, not a uniform, and make sure you are on time First Sergeant," George Lott ordered

"Ok boss," Jim replied, "But I don't have to like it, do I?

"No," Sergeant Major Lott replied, "Just so long as your attitude remains between you and me."

Jim and SSG Carol Anderson arrive at the formal function on time and Jim quietly admitted to himself she was the prettiest female there! Jim and Carol merged into the reception line and waited their turn to greet the General and wish him the best in retirement. As they approached the General, his Sergeant Major looked Jim in the eye and smiled as if to say "Gotcha." Jim returned the smile in an effort to hide his discomfort.

When Jim and Carol reached the General, Jim handed the Sergeant Major his card. Clearly printed on the front of the business cards was the inscription "James E Knight, First Sergeant, 261st Signal Company."

The sergeant major looked at the card, handed it to the General, and announced, "General, may I introduce First Sergeant and Mrs. Jim Knight from the 261st Signal Company."

The general took Carol's hand in his and smiled broadly.

"Oh, Carol," the General replied, "I did not know you were married."

"Neither did I," Carol responded.

The smile on the Sergeant Major's faced dropped to his knees like a ton of bricks.

Again, the General spoke, directing his remarks toward Jim, "First Sergeant, General Thompson told me all about you. Congratulations on the fine job you have done for us. But I thought you were also single," he finished with a questioning look on his face.

Jim smiled weakly as the situation became more awkward by the moment.

"So did I, sir," he replied.

Attempting to recover, the Sergeant Major moved slightly closer to the General and said, "I can explain all this later, sir."

But it was too late, the General looked at the Sergeant Major saying, "I thought you knew the soldiers in this command better than I do? Apparently not."

Jim and Carol quickly moved along to make room for the next couple in line.

"What the hell was that all about?" Jim asked as they moved to the bar for a drink.

"Since when does a General officer address a Staff Sergeant by her first name?" Jim asked firmly.

"Since when?" Carol asked with a stern look on her face "Well, if you must know, since I was his enlisted aid back at Fort Bragg. I held the job for two years before coming over here. He promoted me to Staff Sergeant just before I left."

"Wow," Jim replied. "Looks to me like the Sergeant Major stuck it to himself." Jim said with a wide grin.

"If he didn't like you before now, it's for sure you are not going to be best friends from here on," Carol quipped with a smile.

"You're right about that, but what the hell can he do? Send me to Germany and make me First Sergeant of a big signal company?" Jim replied, trying to hold back the laughter.

"Thank you, Sergeant Anderson… Carol" Jim said in earnest. "I hope the conduct of your senior NCOs has not been too much of an embarrassment to you."

From there on, the remainder of the evening was a grand affair enjoyed by all.

At long last, the pressure was off. The hard work was finished and Jim, along with the rest of the company staff, began to live what might be described as a normal, day-to-day army lifestyle. Jim and his managers were proud of what they had done. Now it was time to sit back and watch success drive the train of day-to-day business for the company. Once Jim was satisfied his organization would function with or without his oversight, Carolyn kept her promise of an extended visit. This was an excellent opportunity to test the process he had initiated by walking away for a while and appointing another NCO to temporarily fill in for him.

Jim and Carolyn took off on a whirlwind tour of Europe. The Bavarian Alps, Austria, Switzerland, and Paris all had their share of Carolyn's two-week visit. The personal side of this adventure was both successful and relaxing for Jim. Carolyn turned out to be the sweetheart of the company. Everyone wanted to meet the first sergeant's sweetheart. She won their hearts almost immediately. The professional test was also totally successful. After the vacation was over, Carolyn returned to the States and Jim resumed the reins of company manager. Jim attended a meeting with Sergeant Major Lott and the other First Sergeants of the battalion shortly after his return. During the business meeting, Jim commented on his vacation, drawing a remark from the Sergeant Major.

"Oh, were you away, First Sergeant? I didn't miss you at all!"

This was music to Jim's ears, but the message was loud and clear. George Lott was not one to offer a lot of praise, but in this case, his apparent off-the-cuff remark has a definite hidden meaning.

The remainder of the tour went well. As the end grew closer, Captain Norman asked Jim to remain just three more months so they could go out together.

"Don't make me get used to a new First Sergeant," he pleaded. "You and I have come too far together. We were sent her for a specific purpose and together, we did what had to be done. It seems only reasonable that we came in together, we should go out together," he said with a frown on his face.

Jim knew he could not refuse the request. He had enjoyed a very close relationship with his Commander and together they had moved mountains.

"Okay Captain," Jim answered, "We will go out together, but you are going to take the heat from Carolyn," Jim replied. "She is ready for the wedding and so am I. On the other hand, I suppose three more months will not make a lot of difference," he concluded.

The next morning Jim sat at his desk trying to figure out how he was going to tell Carolyn about a three-month extension and gain her support at the same time.

As a cloud of gloom grew in his mind, the company clerk rushed through the door announcing, "First Sergeant, Washington is on the line for you," he said breathlessly.

"Washington?" Jim replied.

"Washington who?" Jim asked, visibly irritated by the sudden interruption.

"I don't know who, he would not say," the clerk replied. "All I know is he said this is the White House, Washington, D.C. and I want to talk to Jim Knight, **NOW,**" the clerk sputtered.

Jim grabbed the phone and snapped, "First Sergeant!"

The voice on the other end was calm and steady, "Well, hi there. Do I have their attention? Bet the fact you received a call from the White House will spread all over Germany by tonight," the almost familiar voice said.

A smile filled Jim's face as the memories fell into place. "Trevor, where are you and what in the hell are you doing?"

"Ha," Trevor replied, "Heard that before! I knew you would not forget your old friend. I am cleaning out my desk here at the White House. I served a tour of duty with the White House communications agency and now I am moving back to the army personnel center waiting for my retirement to come through," Trevor announced with a hint of pride in his voice.

"I suppose you are going to tell me you are once again my career manager, my tour is up, and it's time to come home," Jim asked pleadingly.

"Exactly," Trevor replied. "I would have waited till I got back to Alexandria to make this call, but as usual, you have gummed-up the works. In case I forget to tell you later, the list is not released yet and you didn't hear this from me, but you have been selected to attend the Sergeant Majors Academy in Texas for six months, then it's off to Japan where you will get your own battalion," Trevor explained.

"Not possible," Jim chided, "I am not a Sergeant Major, remember?"

"Oh," came the reply, "Did I leave something out? The E9 Board just adjourned and your name is on the list. The initial list is going through the approval process, but you are solid and near the top. You will be a Staff Sergeant Major within three months, then we will convert you to Command Sergeant Major when you leave for Japan. Congratulations, old friend," Trevor said.

"When I looked at my workload last night, I saw your name pop up for reassignment and frankly, was not sure how you were going to react to the academy and a three-year tour in Japan so close on the heels of a two-year tour in Germany," Trevor explained.

"So, I decided I would call you first thing this morning, your time, to make sure all this stuff was acceptable to you before pushing the paperwork any further down the road," Trevor reasoned.

Jim smiled, warmed by the thought that his career had been a success, but now it was time to get a grip on things before they got out of hand.

"Thanks," Jim replied. "But I need one more big favor from you. I need you to tell the army, in an acceptable way, I am going to retire. I will decline both the assignment and the promotion. It is time for me to get back into George Mason University on a full-time basis, get married, and start acting like a husband and father. I gotta go, old friend."

"Hmm," Trevor replied, "Sounds like you are ready for a new start. Second career on the horizon?""Yep," Jim replied. "I am not sure how all this will work, but that is the plan. For most of my adult life I have been in night school preparing for a second career, so I suppose now is the time for me to make that change."

"Me too," Trevor offered. "I am going back to Augusta, Georgia and start a second career as a civilian. You may be interested to know I am on that same promotion list with you and I have already declined," Trevor announced.

"I suspect Patsy will be glad to have an opportunity at playing the full-time wife and staying in one place for more than a short while,"

Jim speculated. "Last time I talked to her, she said living like a gypsy was getting a bit old. Congratulations old friend. You have certainly earned this retirement," Jim said affectionately.

"Thanks pal," Trevor replied. "I will submit all your paperwork from this end and I will make sure the army accepts your wishes and desires. Make sure your retirement request gets into the chain as quickly as possible," Trevor requested.

"I'm asking for a date of March 1st," Jim replied. "I will mail you an advanced copy. Thanks for the help and I will find you when I get back. I owe you pal!" Jim offered.

"See ya," Trevor said, ignoring Jim's comment, "Have a good trip home."

Jim hung up and smiled to himself.

"This career is over," he said to himself. *Now it's on to Act II, whatever that is,* he thought as he walked into Captain Norman's office to chat.

Before he could count the days, he was walking off the aircraft at Dulles Airport and at the end of the gate stood a tall, pretty lady in a short pink dress with outstretched arms. "I'm gonna frame that dress one of these days," he said aloud as he walked toward Carolyn.

Jim was scheduled to retire in one week at Ft. Myer, Virginia. Everything had gone like clockwork. The army had offered a retirement parade complete with hundreds of troops dressed in their Class A uniforms, an honor guard, and a marching band, but Jim declined.

"I have marched in so many retirement parades over the past twenty-one years that I can't count them all, but I will not be responsible for causing the troops to come out on a cold February day just to see me retire. I would prefer a simple handshake from a personnel officer and a long walk to the parking lot," Jim had said.

As Jim walked away from the retirement ceremony, he muttered under his breath, "First Sergeant Franklin, we are done. I kept my promise to you and did the best I could. Thanks for always being there with me. The changing of the guard is completed once again. I hope you know how grateful I am for your guiding hand."

As Jim slid into the driver seat of his car, he thought to himself, *It is now time for Act II to begin!*

Chapter IX

With retirement completed, the first item on Jim and Carolyn's priority list was crossed off. For the first time in twenty years, Jim was unemployed and ready to start a new chapter in life. But as the new adventure started, fate stepped in with a vengeance. Cot, Carolyn's father, died suddenly of a heart attack. While his health had not been the best, there had been little or no hint of a serious problem. Geraldine buried Cot in the town of his birth, Oakland, Maryland, on the top of a mountain overlooking his childhood home.

"He always enjoyed that view," Geraldine commented. "Now he has it for all time."

Jim's daughter Lori Ann married her childhood boyfriend Frank so that seemed to answer the question: "What's going on with Lori these days?" After the wedding, Ann said Frank had joined the navy and was trying to get his act together. At this point in his life, Frank was pretty much a loser. He had finally flunked out of high school, had more than one run-in with local law enforcement, and had started dabbling with drugs and alcohol. From all appearances, Frank was running down the road to hell as fast as he could.

"Sounds like a familiar story," Jim commented. "I seem to remember another young man who joined the military in the hopes of a fresh start and a better outcome than the one he was facing.""Yes," Ann responded, "I seem to remember you were running down that same road to hell at break-neck speed, but I always took credit for getting you on the straight and narrow."

Jim knew better than start something at this late date, so he simply replied, "Yes ma'am, you certainly do deserve a lot of credit. Now you and I can only hope Frank and Lori will not follow our example and perhaps Lori can steer Frank to the straight and narrow. I suspect the military will also play a real active role in his rehabilitation," he said as he walked away from a situation growing worse by the minute.

Fortunately, Ann did not catch his smart remark. Jim had already come down really hard on Ann for not exercising better control over Allen's behavior and paying more attention to his grades in school.

"You better get a grip on Allen or I will," Jim had ordered.

Allen was having severe disciplinary problems. He was skipping school, his grades were down, and he was running with a crowd that Jim did not approve of. That conversation had not gone well and Ann was still very angry about Jim's strong-arm tactics. But Jim knew there was no other solution. One or both parents needed to step in with a firm hand or Allen could be lost. He did not know it then, but within a few weeks, Allen would be relocating to live with him and Carolyn. Allen was on the verge of failing in his junior year of high school and there was no way Jim was going to sit back and watch that happen. Allen had too much promise to allow his talents and potential to go undeveloped.

When the move actually happened, Jim was a bit surprised that Ann let it pass without resistance. Perhaps she was at the end of her rope and simply did not know how to deal with the problem. After a serious father-to-son conversation, Allen began to improve immediately. Jim enrolled Allen in Fairfax High School and the transplant was a complete success. Jim and Allen had always been close, perhaps this was the medicine needed to cure the ailment.

Jim took a firm stand with his son "If I have to accompany you to every class, you will attend, perform well and you will graduate!"

Apparently that was more than enough to turn Allen around. For some reason Jim never really understood, Allen's grades improved dramatically, his attitude was very positive, and he seemed very family oriented.

Moving down the priority list, Jim enrolled in the summer semester at George Mason University and again was on the road toward a degree. He had changed his major from business to secondary education with a minor in biology. That would mean a lot of make-up work. While he had successfully completed the larger part of business study, this curriculum change set him back to making up required courses for the education and biology curriculum, but that was okay with Jim. Now he was a full-time college student at the tender young age of thirty-eight. He was excited about the change and enjoying his life.

On April 25th, perhaps the most important item on the priority list was completed. Jim and Carolyn were married at the Ft. Myer Ceremonial Chapel. Allen and Mike served as best men while Robin was Carolyn's matron of honor. After a short reception, Jim and Carolyn drove to Williamsburg for a short honeymoon. From there, the family settled into the normal, routine lifestyle they all had dreamed about for so long.

Carolyn's career continued to be filled with success after success. All three kids were doing well in school and Jim's studies were rewarded with a grade-point average that placed him on the dean's list. Carolyn made sure he did not forget her GPA was a solid 4.0.

"Yea, yea, I know," Jim said. "That 'C' in accounting did not help. I suppose I am not accustomed to a world where the rules can change that suddenly. Perhaps that is why I like science so much – it won't change tomorrow."

Money was a bit tight with Carolyn the only working member of the family, but Jim's retirement helped pay the bills while the G.I. bill paid his college expenses. Everything remained relatively stable until Robin and Allen graduated from high school and started their freshman year in college. Allen went to George Mason University while Robin chose Old Dominion University in Norfolk.

Jim had been coaching little league baseball since returning from Germany. He enjoyed working with kids and the activity served as a small distraction from his studies and concerns about an ever-tightening financial burden the family was living under. Mike was a very promising pitcher with the ability to throw a baseball at 98 miles per hour and doing it all day without getting tired. Considering he was only twelve years old that was quite a feat, especially when his incredible accuracy was figured into the equation. While Mike's reputation as an up-and-coming young pitcher spread quickly, Jim's reputation as a pitching coach did not go without notice. He developed close relationships with the other coaches and often spent many an hour after the game talking to them about past experiences at work and on the baseball field.

Meanwhile, the financial strain at home grew worse. At the end of the day, paying college expenses for two kids with only one steady income was reaching the point of overwhelming.

Jim and Carolyn discussed alternatives, but both of them knew the only answer was for Jim to drop out of school and get a job. Almost on cue, the phone rang early one Monday morning offering a surprise solution.

"Hi," the cheerful voice at the other end began. "My name is Jim Beam and I am the Washington District Manager for General Telecommunications and Electronics," he continued. "An employee of mine, Bill Hemming, has told me you have all the experience and skills I am looking for in a Project Engineer. Would you be interested in coming in to talk to me about it?" he asked pleadingly.

"Mr. Beam, Bill Hemming and I coach baseball together. I am delighted to hear he is trying to help my second career get started," Jim replied. "I regret to tell you, however, while I have a lot of experience as a Project Manager, I am not an engineer."

"Oh yes," Jim Beam replied, "I completely understand that. Actually, the title is Project Engineer, but the functionality is that of a Project Manager and from what Bill says, you are exactly what I am looking for. Won't you come in and talk to me?" he asked again.

Jim's mind was racing. *Hell,* he thought to himself, *I have never held a civilian job, much less interviewed for one,* he thought to himself.

"Yes, Mr. Beam," Jim replied. "I will come talk to you but keep in mind, I just recently retired from the army and I must admit my experience in industry and the commercial world is somewhat limited," Jim offered.

"Even better," Jim Beam replied. "I understand you are a retired army First Sergeant. You may be surprised to learn that your technical skills coupled with the character of a First Sergeant is right on target. I need some fresh ideas around here to help me solve a few business problems and my understanding is that you specialize in that area. Is tomorrow too soon?" he asked.

"Nine o'clock?"

"I'll be there Mr. Beam and thanks for the call," Jim replied as he replaced the phone on the receiver. "Carolyn is not going to believe this," Jim said out loud to the empty room.

The next morning, Jim dressed in his best blue, pen-striped suit with a freshly starched white shirt and a burgundy tie. *Might as well play the game,* he thought as he drove off to the appointment.

The interview went well. Jim Beam went to great lengths providing a detailed description of the Project Engineer duties and responsibilities. Jim kept waiting for the hard part. As Jim Beam patiently explained every small detail, Jim kept thinking, *When I was on active duty, I did this kind of work as an additional duty. I wonder when he is going to get to the real job.*

Finally, Jim Beam leaned back in his chair, obviously pleased with his presentation, smiled at Jim, and asked, "Any questions about any of this?"*I can't believe he is finished,* Jim thought to himself. *I suppose I need to ask a question, even though I completely understand everything he said.*

Jim quickly asked several questions about the company's marketing organization, career opportunities, technical training on the GTE product line, then closed with a question about call processing in their smaller telephone systems. *That should do it,* he thought to himself.

Jim Beam was all smiles. After a brief discussion of Jim's technical background, technical training, and experiences as an instructor at the army signal school, Jim Beam knew he had the right man for the job.

"Will you fly to Chicago tomorrow to talk to our vice president?" Jim Beam asked.

"He is going to be very anxious to talk to you."

"Hmm yes," Jim replied. "As you may know, I am a full-time college student working on a degree and we are on a short academic break. Yes, I can go to Chicago if you wish."

From the minute the plane arrived in Chicago, the red carpet was out. Jim was totally surprised at the treatment he received. The Vice President, Mr. Reatta, was more than generous with his time and went to great lengths explaining career opportunities offered by GTE. The day was filled with discussion of the GTE product line, expected corporate growth, and the many advantages brought to a GTE professional. Jim was truly impressed.

As he boarded the aircraft for the return trip to Washington, Mr. Reatta said, "You will hear from our director of personnel in a day or so. Have a good trip home and give my best to Jim Beam when you see him."*Sure I will,*

Jim thought *If they really wanted him to work for GTE, someone would have made an offer. They did not! I suppose Mr. Reatta did not like what he saw*, Jim thought to himself. *I have heard that line before - you will hear from us soon. Soon usually never comes.*

"Oh well, in the end it was a great experience. I may not have landed the job, but I sure did enjoy the interview," Jim said to himself with a smile of satisfaction on his face as he settled in the soft, first class seat of the jet liner.*I wonder what went wrong? Truth is, I could do that job with my hands tied behind my back. Wonder what it pays?* Jim wondered

The next few days were filled with end of semester exams and Jim was too busy to give the interview much thought. In fact, he told Carolyn not to expect anything because if they had wanted him, they would have asked. The fact that they did not seems to point to a failed attempt, Jim had reasoned. But all was not lost, Jim had a three-week break before the next semester started, perhaps he would start looking at the want ads.

Two days later, the unexpected phone call came. Carolyn had come home at noon to take Robin to a dental appointment and Jim had been cutting the lawn. As they sat at the kitchen table eating their lunch, the phone rang and Jim picked it up.

"Mr. Knight, This is Tim Johnson at GTE Chicago. I am the Director of Personnel Services and I am calling to offer you a position as a Project Engineer with our Washington District Office."

Jim motioned at Carolyn and pointed to the phone. He formed the letters "GTE" with his lips and smiled. Carolyn's face immediately lit up with a big smile.

"Yes Mr. Johnson," Jim replied. "How are things in Chicago?"

"Actually, Mr. Knight, everything here will be just fine if I can convince you to become one of our Project Engineers," he replied. "I apologize for not calling you sooner, but things have been a bit hectic here as we are trying to wrap up negotiation with our labor union and renewal of the contract."

For the next ten minutes, Tim Johnson went through all the boiler plate required to offer Jim a position as a Project Engineer.

At the end of his lengthy dissertation, Mr. Johnson asked, "Are you willing to accept the position, Mr. Knight?"

"Please, call me Jim," he responded. "And what is the annual salary?" Jim asked.

When Tim Johnson gave him the number, Jim dropped the phone in shock.

After quickly picking up the phone again, he heard Tim Johnson say, "Is there something wrong with that salary? Our policy is that after six months of performance, you will be evaluated then considered for a substantial raise, but we need to make sure you are going to perform as well as we think," Tim Johnson reasoned.

Jim looked across the table and winked. Carolyn's face was drawn with concern and disappointment. It was clear she thought the salary was very low. Jim smiled at her, formed a fist with his right hand, and held his thumb in the air.

"Yes, Mr. Johnson," Jim replied with a smile on his face. "The salary is fine and I will accept your offer. What happens next?" Jim replied, trying not to reveal his joy and enthusiasm.

"I will get a letter out to you today making the offer formal and you should hear from Jim Beam by tomorrow. He will give you all the details you need. Thank you, Mr. Knight, I will personally inform Mr. Reatta and Mr. Beam of your acceptance. I know they will be delighted. Welcome aboard!" he said as the conversation ended.

Jim leaned over the table and whispered the salary number in her ear. Suddenly, her face brightened with a smile from ear to ear.

"You must be joking," she said as tears began to fill her eyes. She jumped into Jim's arms and wrapped her arms around his neck saying "Baby, we have finally arrived!"

Before they could get through their conversation, the phone rang again, this time, Jim Beam's voice was loud and obviously pleased.

"Welcome to GTE," he said. "I know you have a number of details to take care of so why not take the rest of the week off and I will see you in my office at eight o'clock on Monday morning. Is that okay with you?"

"Yes sir," Jim replied. "That will work well."

Jim had a good feeling about this new job and his new boss. He liked Jim Beam right away. He did not know it at the time, but Monday morning would begin a new friendship that would last a lifetime.

The first two weeks were filled with product orientation training in the company's Chicago manufacturing facility, then it was down to business. Jim was surprised at how closely the processes and procedures he had used in the military paralleled those of the company. When he ran into situations where company procedures did not seem adequate or were non-existent, he simply used those he had learned in the military and kept going. What he did not realize was that those around him saw the solutions he applied and immediately tagged him as an innovative problem solver.

"If you had asked permission on this one," Jim Beam said more than once, "I might not have agreed. But in the end, you solved a tough problem and did it well. It's difficult to argue with success," he would say.

Everything Jim and Carolyn had planned was moving along like a well scripted, long rehearsed play. The children were doing well in school. Robin and Allen were straight "A" college students and Mike was getting good grades in high school.

Jim often talked to the kids about being high achievers in school.

"You guys can be at the top of your class. You are smart. Never do just enough to get by," Jim said time after time. "Always go one step beyond what is expected and you will always be successful. Take that from one who learned that lesson the hard way."

Jim knew this phase of their lives could well be the most important of all. Now was the time they formed the habits that would more than likely guide their behavior as adults. Jim knew achievement at this level would foster desires for even greater success when their school days were over.

Carolyn's job was also moving along really well. After a tour as a Program Analyst, Mr. Simmonds promoted her to the position of Management Analyst and moved her into the agency's manpower management division. *Each day, that gap in her experience closes and she moves closer to the top of the totem pole,* Mr. Simmonds thought to himself. *Someday real soon, she will be ready to assume management of one of my branch offices and from there, well, my retirement is getting close,* He silently planned.

The next year passed quickly while success after success piled up for Jim and Carolyn. Their concerns about income soon dissolved as promotions, raises, and bonuses swelled their bank account.

"Seems we made the right decisions along the way," Carolyn often commented. "We could not have planned this any better."But fate was still lurking in the background. When the boys invited their cigarette-smoking friends to join them on the back porch one warm summer afternoon after school, no one could have forecasted the horrible results. The sparks from a cigarette had fallen onto a cushion of the sofa, smoldered for hours, then, just as dinner was being served at 7:00, burst into flames. The fire quickly spread into the roof of the house before the fire department could bring it under control.

The next three months were spent in a temporary townhouse while the house was being repaired and restored. In the end, the house and family were all the better for the ordeal as the repairs had dramatically improved the overall condition and appearance of a house that was more than twenty-five years of age. The family took the minor crisis in stride and ignored the inconvenience of a temporary relocation. A romantic would have argued that fate was offended. A good attempt to interrupt the family's trip toward a greater level of happiness and prosperity had failed miserably.

As his first year with the company drew to a close, Jim's boss, Jim Beam, decided to make changes in the structure of the service center that promised to improve productivity and profitability of the organization. After a tough week, Jim Beam asked Jim to stay late on a Friday evening to talk about the business.

"I have been struggling with a big problem in this organization for quite some time that I just could not solve," Jim Beam said as the two of them settled into comfortable chairs in the conference room.

"The problem is," Jim Beam said "while we have our engineering organization under control and Bill Cormack is working well as our manager of adds, moves, and changes for the installed customer base, our installation act is worse than terrible," he concluded with a look of frustration on his face. "As if that isn't enough, I feel terribly uncomfortable about our logistics organization and the warehouse."

The room grew awkwardly quiet for a few moments as the two of them stared at each other across the table.

Jim smiled at his boss and replied, "It's a shame the company is not organized to allow a Service Manager in this office," he offered. "If you had the position, you could reorganize by placing the installation group, logistics, and service work order group under the service manager while you retained control of the engineering function. That would take some of the load off you, give you an assistant, and allow that service manager to concentrate on improvement of the installation process," Jim offered. "You might even want to designate the senior engineer as lead Engineer and assign him or her a few supervisory duties."

Jim Beam smiled as he leaned across the table. He folded his hands in front of him and seemed to be choosing his words carefully.

"That is exactly what I told Tony Reatta, last week," Jim Beam offered. "He said he liked the idea and funding was available, but he did not have a service manager elsewhere in the company he could reassign into the position." Jim Beam said as he leaned back in his chair with a look of dismay on his face.

"Hmm," Jim replied. "And all for the loss of a horseshoe nail," Jim replied prophetically. "I thought there were a fair number of capable people waiting for a promotion into the management ranks."

"Not quite," Jim Beam replied. "Tony suggested I promote you. He said your record is loaded with experience as a technician and successful manager. Tony seems to think you are a natural for the job." Jim Beam offered with a big smile on his face.

Jim was surprised, but managed to hold his matter-of-fact expression as he replied, "You can't be serious about making someone a manager in this organization when they only have one year of service with the company. You forget my last full-time job was that of a First Sergeant in the army. Industry operates a bit differently than the U.S. Army," Jim offered.

Jim Beam smiled as he leaned forward. "Not good enough, my friend," he replied. "You took to your current job like a duck to water. It is clear to all of us that you did this kind of work for the army with both hands tied behind your back. You have quietly demonstrated the need to improve some of our engineering practices and introduced procedures that make the entire engineering process more efficient and cost effective. My sense is that you need a bit more challenge in your work," Jim Beam offered.

Now Jim was surprised. He came into the meeting thinking he would simply be part of a brain-storming exercise and leaves with a promotion - a big promotion.

"Is there a salary increase?" Jim inquired

"Twenty-thousand a year salary increase, a management level expense account, and the new title is free," Jim Beam offered without hesitation.

Jim did not have to think about it.

"Done," he replied. "When do I start?" he asked

"Monday morning," Jim Beam replied. "I will call the staff together, make the announcement, then you can get to work. In the meantime, decide how you want to realign the organization and I will do the spade work with Tony and the corporate gurus," Jim Beam said as he rose to his feet "Your marching orders are, fix our installation and logistics problems, make them profitable, and while you are at it, make sure all our customers are happy." Jim Beam replied

"Okay boss," Jim replied "I suppose that gives me something to think about this weekend," Jim said as they walked out of the office together.

"See you Monday Mr. Service Manager," Jim Beam said with a smile as he opened the door to his car.

The weeks and months passed quickly. Jim quickly pulled the installation and logistics organizations under his control and began the healing process. In a very short time, installation was making a profit, logistics was running smoothly, and customer endorsements were rolling in. Life looked good and the often cruel acts of fate were nowhere in sight!

Then one bright Monday morning in early September, the world stood still! In the office early, as usual, Jim had the installation teams on the road, received a briefing from Bill Cormack on service order plans for the week, and Jim was ready to brief the boss, as soon as he filled his coffee cup. Jim jumped to his feet from behind his desk and immediately felt the room spin around him.

"Hmm, got to my feet a bit too fast," he told himself as he leaned against the wall to steady himself. But the dizziness did not stop. He could feel perspiration on his face, excessive perspiration, and his knees felt weak. The chair behind his desk seemed miles away as his mind raced to figure out what to do next.

Out of nowhere, Bill Cormack appeared at his side.

"You look terrible, boss," he said. "Are you okay?" he asked as he took a firm grip on Jim's arm."

"No!" Jim replied, "Something is wrong. Help me get to my desk," he asked.

As Jim sat down behind his desk, he felt worse. Now he felt like he had run up a very long hill without stopping. He was short winded and breathing became increasingly difficult.

"Think I better go home till whatever this is passes," Jim announced.

"Okay," Bill Cormack replied. "Leave your car here, I will drive you home and have the secretary call Carolyn telling her to meet us at your place," he said. "I suspect you may need some help as the day progresses," Bill speculated.

Jim and Bill piled into the car and Bill sped off toward Jim's home. As the trip progressed, Jim felt even worse. Breathing became more and more labored and pain in the upper part of both arms quickly set in. Bill had been watching Jim carefully as the trip progressed. Suddenly, he made a sharp right turn across two lanes of traffic and into a driveway marked "Ambulance Entrance".

Bill quickly wrestled Jim out of the car and into the emergency room of Doctors Commonwealth Hospital.

As they came through the door Bill called out in a loud voice, "Can I have some help over here? We have a heart attack in progress!"

As the strong arms of two orderlies grabbed each of Jim's arms, the world went black. Jim passed out! When he awoke, he was in an uncomfortable bed, needles and tubes were everywhere, the heart monitor mounted next to his head kept a steady, loud beat, and Carolyn was standing at the foot of the bed watching him. Her face was drawn and she had obviously been crying.

"Hi, Sugar bear," Jim said weakly. "What the hell is going on?" he asked.

Carolyn walked around the bed, gently held his hand in hers and said, "You have had a heart attack. You scared the hell out of all of us," she said timidly, trying to force a smile.

"The doctors kept saying they caught it in time and stopped the heart attack, but you would not wake up," she said.

"How do you feel?" she asked.

"Tired," Jim replied. "I feel like I been dragged face-down behind a truck for a mile or two," he said, trying to make a joke.

Carolyn did not laugh.

Almost on cue, an emergency room doctor came into the room and stood beside the bed. He glanced at the equipment, then smiled at Jim.

Directing his comments to Carolyn, he said, "He is going to be fine. We are going to give him a sedative to make him sleep, he needs lots of rest. In an hour or so, we will transport him to Fairfax Hospital. They have the best heart unit on the east coast. They will run some tests and tell you what the next step will be, but I think he is going to be like new in a very short time." He patted Jim on the head and smiled as he walked past Carolyn to leave the room.

Right behind him, a nurse walked up to the bed, gave Jim an injection and as she walked away, fade to black again!

Chapter X

Recovery began almost immediately. Fortunately, quick thinking doctors at the emergency room administered the right treatments at the right time and damage to Jim's heart was minimal. A little rest combined with a few recuperative processes such as physical therapy and an improved diet worked miracles. When all was said and done, the improved diet was the tough part. The switch to fruits and veggies and away from chocolate chip cookies, potatoes, and sugar-loaded foods took a while, but eventually it worked out for the best. Jim felt better with each passing day.

Jim Beam dropped by to visit as often as he could. He reported that Bill Cormack was holding down the fort nicely with the processes and procedures Jim had put in place, but the company was anxious for Jim to recover and return to work.

"I promise we will miss you," Jim Beam remarked. "But don't let that go to your head. The company provides twenty-six weeks of paid recovery, so take your time. When you and your doctor are ready, give me a call. In the meantime, we will stay in contact with Carolyn just to make sure she has all she needs and, at the same time, make sure you do not become too much of a baby while recovering."

"Sounds good to me," Jim remarked. "You know how us guys can be such big babies when we get sick. I'll try not to become too much of a pain…Thanks boss," Jim replied.

After eight weeks, Jim's Cardiologist sent him back to work for half days. Twelve weeks later, Jim was back to the nine to five grind. His health was good because he followed his doctor's orders to the letter. An improved diet – low fat and low sugar – combined with an ongoing program of exercise and physical conditioning made a world of difference. Jim joked that he was only following doctor's orders by playing golf a lot more often.

Jim continued to refine his service processes and procedures in the hope of improving service quality and profitability at the same time. The process was slow because too much of one could easily jeopardize the other but as time passed, the delicate balance worked well and both goals were achieved. At the same time, Jim implemented a 100% accountability process into the logistics department and after many painful inventories and inventory adjustments, the process proved effective. Once again, Jim felt comfortable enough to sit back and watch the operations run on its own momentum.

It wasn't long before Jim Beam was selected for an executive position elsewhere in the company. Jim felt very uncomfortable about working for a new boss. His relationship with Jim Beam had always been a good one and they had worked together well. Jim learned a great deal about the business from his boss and was always very appreciative of the special efforts Jim Beam often made to improve his understanding of the commercial business world.

Late one Friday afternoon, Jim Beam called Jim into his office for what Jim thought would be a routine, end of the week business discussion about workloads, customer concerns, and all the things two business managers worried a lot about. This meeting had become a part of their business week and always resulted in a clear slate of action needed to start the next business week. Jim walked into his boss's office with his notepad, prepared to discuss a number of business topics.

"Close the door and lose the notebook," Jim Beam said as Jim walked into the room.

Jim dropped the notebook on a table, gently closed the door, and took a seat on the sofa across from Jim Beam's desk.

"Okay, boss," Jim said with a smile, "I'll bite, what's up?"

Jim Beam leaned across his desk, folded his hands and looked Jim right in the eye with a very serious look on his face.

"I'm out of here in another week or so," he said calmly. "Our vice president has nominated you as my replacement," he continued.

"Whoa," Jim replied with a look of surprise on his face. "I never even imagined I would be a candidate," he said with a concerned look. "I have only been with this company a couple years and I know there are quite a few eligible, well qualified, managers in this company with a lot more seniority, waiting for a job like this one," Jim said as if trying to remind Jim Beam of his junior status.

"Yea, yea, yea," Jim Beam replied. "We have considered all that, but you are missing a few very important points," Jim Beam argued as he leaned back in his chair.

"This is the only service center in the company making a profit! This is the only service center with a customer acceptance rating in excess of ninety-five percent! And, as if that isn't enough, all those other managers, the ones you consider to be top candidates for this position, have been trying to figure out how to convince you to move out of the Washington D.C. area and come to work for them," Jim said with a big smile.

"We are all convinced you are a great Service Manager, now it is time for you to lead the parade. And before you start crying about your tenure with this company, let me remind you the experience and training you have as an army First Sergeant is far greater than anything any manager in this company has. Most of them sat around waiting for something to happen, while you and your subordinate managers take it upon themselves to make things happen. Not only are you more than qualified for this job, I could build a good argument saying you may be a bit overqualified, especially considering the amount of college credit you have earned in night school," Jim Beam said with a chuckle.

"The answer here is real simple," Jim Beam continued. "Either you take the job and continue the good work you started here or someone else comes in and starts doing everything his or her way. I can almost guarantee you that will not be fun!" Jim Beam concluded.

Jim leaned back with a look of complete surprise still on his face. While he had hoped someday to move up a notch or two, he had thought that would not happen for at least another five years or so. Now, it was suddenly decision time and Jim was totally unprepared.

"That's quite a speech boss," Jim replied. "Am I required to give you an answer right now or can I have thirty seconds to think about all this?" Jim asked.

Jim Beam smiled. "You have all the time in the world. Think about it over the weekend. Talk to Carolyn about it. I would bet she will get your head on straight and tell you to take the job, "

Jim Beam concluded as he stood up and held out his hand.

"Thanks boss," Jim said. "I know you had a heavy hand in this, so thanks for the support. I'll talk to you on Monday," Jim said as he shook his boss's hand and then walked to his car.

When Jim arrived home, Carolyn was sitting at the kitchen table with a glass of wine in front of her. Her face was drawn with concern.

"Hi Sugar bear," Jim called as he walked into the kitchen. "You are never going to believe what has happened," Jim said again, noticing a very serious expression on Carolyn's face.

"Wow," Jim exclaimed. "Why the down-in-the-mouth look?" he asked as he sat down across from her. "Bad day at the office?" Jim chided.

"I know you will find this hard to believe," Carolyn said as she looked up at Jim, "But Mr. Simmonds called me into his office today and told me effective Monday morning, I am promoted to GM-13 and will take over as Deputy Chief of the Manpower Division."

Carolyn looked like she was almost in tears. "I just can't believe it," she kept saying.

Jim reached out and took her hand in his. "Sugar bear, that is wonderful news. Why the long face? You should be the happiest girl in town," Jim said pleadingly.

"Oh, I am," Carolyn said managing a weak smile "The problem is, I think some of the others in our organization are so much more deserving and I feel like I have been given a job that should have gone to someone else more deserving than me," she explained.

"Can this be happening twice in the same day?" Jim said quietly.

"Twice in the same day?" Carolyn repeated. "I'm not sure what you mean," she asked with a lost look on her face

"Later," Jim said. "But for now, I should not have to remind you that Mr. Simmonds has been preparing you for bigger and better things for a long time. And while that was happening, your contemporaries had more than their fair share of opportunities to prepare themselves for promotions," Jim argued.

"Did you see any of them in night school?" Jim continued. "Did you see any of them taking all those training courses trying to improve their skills?" Jim reasoned. "Hmm, I don't think so," he said firmly.

"Since the beginning you have worked twice as hard, and a lot wiser I might add, than everyone around you because you only wanted to be really good at what you do," Jim continued. "So, you competed and won. Perhaps not intentionally to compete, but none the less, you worked hard at it! That is nothing to be ashamed of, you should be proud as hell! In the end, I bet all of your friends who might have been eligible for that job knew all too well, you were the best choice," Jim said as he clapped his hands in front of Carolyn as if to awaken her from a bad dream.

Carolyn's face brightened and a smile slowly began to appear.

"I knew you would have the right perspective on all this" she said. "Thanks for the coaching. I suppose I just needed a small reminder that you and I have worked so hard to re-establish ourselves since we came together. I think you are right; it is about high time we started to win now and then," she said as the tension and strain disappeared from her face.

"Okay, I got it. Monday morning, I will move into my new office and start acting like a Deputy Chief," Carolyn announced with pride.

"That's my girl," Jim said clapping his hand in applause for her. "Welcome to the world of business managers," he said, offering his hand for a congratulatory handshake.

Jim poured himself a glass of wine and sat down opposite Carolyn with a big smile on his face.

"What were you were saying about twice in the same day?" Carolyn asked with a quizzical look on her face. Jim smiled and leaned across the table as he moved his wine glass closer to her.

"You just said it is about time you and I started winning a few every now and then," Jim explained. " And I really agree. You and I have been scratching our way up from the bottom for a very long time. It is about time the good guys started seeing the fruits of their labor," Jim explained.

"Is there a message somewhere in all that?" Carolyn asked, "Or are you just being philosophical?"

By now, Jim had a real big smile on his face. This very brief conversation with Carolyn had been more than enough to convince him that his own decision was a lot easier than he realized.

He slowly told her about the conversation with Jim Beam earlier that day.

"Are you pulling my leg?" Carolyn asked with a huge smile on her face. "Do you realize while I was in My Simmonds' office being told of my promotion, you were, at the very same time, in Jim Beam's office receiving the same news?" Carolyn explained.

"You did tell Jim you would accept, didn't you?" Carolyn asked with a sudden look of uncertainty.

"Not exactly," Jim shyly confessed. "It was not until we had our little talk a few minutes ago that I realized, I was going to accept the offer to replace Jim Beam," Jim admitted.

Carolyn's face brightened. She held out her wine glass offering a toast.

"To us," she said confidently, "May all our days be as happy and successful as this one," she said, holding her glass out in front of Jim.

Jim picked up his glass and touched hers gently, "Yes ma'am, I'll drink to that all day long!" Jim said. "You once said someday we would reach the other side and our lives would improve. Well, I think today is that day. Someday is getting closer all the time," Jim announced confidently.

From this point, every day that passed was better than the day before. Jim and Carolyn's successes began to pile up. Raises and bonuses seemed to come one on top of another. During a shopping trip, they stumbled upon a house under construction just a few miles away from their neighborhood. The real estate agent advised that the builder had completed the house, but had not sold it because interest rates were much too high. The bank was threatening to foreclose on the builder. After a long talk with their banker and some skillful negotiations with the builder and his banker, Carolyn and Jim bought the new house. Interestingly enough, the new house was located on Prosperity Avenue! It was a beautiful colonial sitting on a one-acre lot with plenty of wooded area behind the house. It boasted four bedrooms, four and a half baths, a workshop in the basement, and a recreation room big enough to get lost in.

"I suppose this means we have arrived after all," Carolyn said as they began to move into their new home.

"It sure is hard to tell the difference between this and success," Jim agreed. "I certainly could argue that we waited long enough for this to happen."

"Do you think we might want to consider a big swimming pool in the backyard?" Carolyn asked, tapping the side of her head as though lost in deep thought.

"Wow," Jim replied. "I had not thought of that. You are right, a swimming pool would be perfect for that lot. I think an in-ground pool with cement decking all around and plenty of room for parties!" Jim speculated.

"Absolutely," Carolyn added, "And following that, I think we need to remodel our recreation room so we have a bar, dance floor, and a big-screen TV at one end."

"Wow," Jim replied, "We just spent a lot of money, sweetheart."

"It's okay, baby," Carolyn said. "From here out, we can well afford it, so why not enjoy the fruits of our hard work?"

All their hopes and dreams came together as if they had been scripted. In the next spring, the swimming pool was completed. With new landscaping in place, it was perfect. The recreation room was remodeled and a large bar was built complete with a wine rack, refrigerator, and a sink for the bartender. Life was really good for the small family. Allen and Robin were in college, Mike was in high school; all three of them were doing well. The next couple of years passed with life treating the small family better and better each day. Jim's business had grown dramatically and because of his success in the Washington district, he was promoted to Regional Service Manager.

"Draw a line from Detroit to the Gulf of Mexico," his boss said during the promotion ceremony. "You are responsible for all company service to the east in that area except Cape Kennedy, New York City, and Boston - they are special contracts," he said.

From there, Jim's days were long and his nights much too short. Every Monday morning he boarded an aircraft, destined for somewhere in his service area, and rarely returned until the following Friday evening or Saturday. He spent every available minute planting the policies and practices that had made him so successful as a Washington District Manager in his new service area. It was not long before the results began to show. Slowly, but surely, profit margins began to increase, customer endorsements were rolling in, and employee morale was high. But Jim was uncomfortable. While his region was doing well, others were not. The sales organization was taking a beating in the market-place, sales were down. Competitors were introducing new equipment with features far surpassing those of Jim's company. Senior managers placed in the other service regions of the company had extensive experience in the data industry, but not the telephone business. Unfortunately, running a telephone business as if it were a data business will not work well in the long term.

When they tried to run the telephone business like a data business, the model began to fail. Jim tried to convince his fellow Regional Managers to use some of his methods, but they were reluctant to try a lot of new methods they did not fully understand. Before long, Jim was riding as high as he could, but the company was failing around him. Unfortunately, his successes were not sufficient to carry the company. Jim began to worry about his future.

"I have worked hard and tried my best to make everything successful. But in the end, I am staring failure right in the teeth," Jim complained to his boss in frustration.

"Hang in there," Jim was told. "Perhaps we can pull this thing out after all. The other two Regional Managers are well experienced and anxious to fix their problems. You focus on keeping your region in good shape and I will make sure the other two start giving you a little competition," his boss said reassuringly.

Then one rare Monday morning, Jim had delayed his weekly travel ritual to handle a serious customer contract problem in the Washington District.

As he sat at his desk studying options to solve the problem, his secretary knocked on the door saying, "Mr. Rudy Gatt on the phone for you. I told him you were in conference, but he insisted saying you would make an exception for him," she said with a questioning look on her face.

"Rudy is correct," Jim said with a smile. "I need a break anyway," he said, reaching for the phone on his desk.

Rudy was a civilian working at the agency. Jim had worked with him a number of times on panels and special study groups. Rudy was a smart, aggressive business manager with a tremendous background in the telephone industry. Jim always knew Rudy would end up at the top of the management ladder, sooner or later.

"Rudy!" Jim said loudly. "It's been a long time. Heard you moved up to the penthouse at the agency."

"Oh yes," Rudy replied. "I have somehow sneaked up the ladder while no one was looking," he calmly offered.

"Chief of operations?" Jim asked as if he did not already know.

"Exactly," Rudy replied. "We have a new Program Manager and he is building a team to completely renovate the world-wide telephone network."

"Wow, big job, but more than overdue," Jim replied. "I am glad to hear you are at the helm. The voice network needs to be brought into the twentieth century," Jim offered calmly.

"Yep," Rudy replied. "It took a lot of work to sell the program to the joint chiefs, but once we did, everything has taken off like a V8 Ford in passing gear."

Jim chuckled. "Lucky you," he said. "And to what do I owe the pleasure of this call? Does this mean you are buying drinks today at happy hour or are you looking for a new contractor?" Jim asked.

"I wish," Rudy said. "I've got too much on my plate. I will be here tonight, just like every other night, until nine, ten, eleven o'clock," Rudy said weakly.

"Sorry pal," Jim replied. "You get no sympathy from me. I've been burning the midnight oil right along with you."

"Okay," Rudy said. "I'll do my crying somewhere else, but the reason I called is to tell you I need a Project Manager to manage the network upgrade in the United States," Rudy said in a measured tone.

"You need someone with a good working knowledge of the government network, but with a lot of experience on the commercial side as well," Jim offered. "I'm not sure I can help you. The only person I know of is Tom Brewster in California and he is very happy with his current job. I heard he was recently promoted to vice president," Jim said, trying to recall where all his old military communications friends had landed after retirement.

"I hear you," Rudy replied, "But I don't need Tom, I need you."

Jim was shocked. He had not for one second interpreted this to be a job offer from his old friend.

"Yes, yes," Rudy continued, "I know you are the Regional Manager and my friends in the industry tell me you are setting the world on fire, but you are the best man for the job and I need to find out if you are interested before I start beating the bushes," Rudy said with a tone of finality. "Besides," Rudy continued, "My industry friends tell me your counterparts in the company are not matching your track record and the company might be in trouble, real soon. I saw that AT&T beat your socks off on the Cape Kennedy bid."

"Heard about that, did you?" Jim replied.

"The rumor is true," Jim confessed. "I can beat their service offering to death, but unfortunately our equipment can't satisfy the government's requirements nearly as well as the AT&T machine," Jim offered.

"But getting back to the matter at hand, I had not thought about coming back to the government," Jim offered. "This is my first real job in industry and frankly, I have been having a real good time. Besides, my salary is a bit high and I do have two kids in college," Jim concluded.

"Oh yea, I know all that," Rudy said in an argumentative tone. "Give me a number."

Jim thought for a moment, added a few numbers to his current salary, then gave Rudy the answer.

Rudy did not hesitate.

"Okay," he said. "I can meet that and add a few bucks to sweeten the deal. Will you think about it?"

Rudy's quick response surprised Jim.

"Sure will," Jim offered, trying to sound matter-of-fact about it.

"How long do I have?" Jim asked.

"I would like to have the new guy here in two weeks or so, if possible," Rudy said. "Take till the end of the week, then let me know."

"Your offer is tempting," Jim said. "Especially the part about working on your team. Let me talk to Carolyn and I'll get back to you and thanks for remembering me," Jim said as the conversation ended.

Jim thought for a moment, then rang his secretary on the intercom.

"Yes sir," came Donna's voice over the speaker system.

"Get my wife on the phone please," Jim asked. "Tell her if she is doing something important to take a break, we need to talk."

"Yes sir," Donna replied.*It just keeps getting better and better*, Jim thought to himself as he waited for Donna to get Carolyn on the phone.

Chapter XI

Jim gently tapped on Rudy's door, causing him to look up from the pile of papers on his desk.

"Hi Jim," Rudy said, "Come on in."

"I waited for your secretary to show up," Jim offered, "But when she did not, I just barged in," he said with a smile.

"Ah yes," Rudy replied. "In fact, she has been real busy arranging reinstatement of your security clearance, organizing your office, and scheduling a meeting this afternoon with our contractors," Rudy said, waving his hand in the air like a magician. "They have put together a briefing that should bring you up to date on the contract for upgrade of the U.S. portion of the network."

"For the time being, I have you reporting to Bill Muncer. He is the overall Operations Manager of our continental U.S and Alaska network. You didn't hear this from me, but pay attention to his role around here, I expect you will assume it in a few months. Bill has announced plans to retire in six months. By then, you should be ready to take the reins," Rudy said with a big smile.

"You didn't mention anything about this is our conversations," Jim said with a sly smile on his face. "Hell, I haven't even started the new job and already I am being promoted," Jim observed.

"Oh yea, you don't know the half of it, but I still have a few loose ends, so let's not talk about that right now," Rudy said with a pleading tone in his voice. "Let's talk about your new position as Project Manager for the U.S. renovation," Rudy said as he leaned back in his chair.

Jim did not fully understand Rudy's comments, but knew there was a confidential message there. Jim let the subject drop as Rudy had suggested. He knew when the time was right, Rudy would bring him on board with the details.

"Works for me," Jim replied. "So what are we going to do in this worldwide network overhaul and how do we get it done?"

Over the next three hours and two pots of coffee, Rudy laid out highlights of the grand plan to completely renovate the entire worldwide network. The joint staff wanted all the new technology, a bigger, more responsive network, and all the bells and whistles that go along with it. Overseas portions of the network would be renovated first, with the U.S. portion as the final phase. In conjunction with the U.S. phase, Jim would be required to negotiate and configure a new gateway to the Canadian military network for contingency purposes. Jim had about two years to finalize the planning, finish design of the U.S portion, select contractors, prepare an implementation plan, and negotiate an agreement with Canada to support the new network.

"You remember Colonel Clark from Ottawa?" Rudy asked.

"No, I don't think so," Jim replied. "I remember a Lt. Colonel Clark who was part of the Canadian switched voice organization," Jim replied quietly as he tried to remember another Clark in the Canadian organization.

"Ah yes," Rudy replied. "He may have been a Lt. Colonel when you worked with him. Well, he is not a Lt. Colonel anymore," Rudy said with a sly smile on his face. "Your Lt. Colonel Roger Clark is now Major General Roger Clark and he is running the entire communications show for the Canadian military," Rudy said, waving his hands in front of him.

"Well," Jim replied. "Roger, oops, make that General Clark and I were close chums working cross-border issues back in those days," Jim said as he recalled the many hours, days, weeks, and months he had spent with Roger in Ottawa.

"I look forward to seeing him again," Jim said with anticipation of renewing an old acquaintance. "Has he changed much?" Jim asked.

"You will see him in two weeks," Rudy replied. "Your staff and General Clark's staff are working the nuts and bolts of a relatively sensitive agreement between Canada and the U.S. Apparently, there are several complex issues to be resolved. I told the joint staff you would put the finishing touches on it for us," Rudy said as he looked up with a pleading look on his face.

"Roger and I share a common interest," Jim offered. "I feel sure we can agree on a plan to ensure that interests of both countries are served," Jim concluded with confidence. "Roger and I are both golfers. He never could beat me, so all I need to do is give him two strokes a side and perhaps that will sweeten the deal," Jim joked.

"I'll leave it to you," Rudy said as he stood up "Now, let me show you around. It might be good to start with your office," said Rudy as he walked up beside Jim and motioned him toward the hallway.

"You briefing will start at 1300 in the main conference room. All the contractor big wigs will be there to help get you started. You should expect to spend at least all afternoon as they have much to say, not to mention a few tough decisions you will be dealing with," Rudy said as they walked side by side to Jim's new office.The months passed quickly. Jim spent a lot of time in Canada as his staff met with General Clark's people. What they did not know was that Jim and General Clark spent a lot of time together as well, mostly on the golf course. While each staff worked the details of the agreement based on direction from their respective boss, Jim and Roger met frequently and had all the tough issues resolved after a few eighteen-hole rounds of golf and many a long evening stroll around the canals of Ottawa.

Days turned to weeks and weeks to months as Jim worked his new job. It was both fun and challenging. Jim was having the time of his life. The great part about this job was that most evenings, Jim went home to Carolyn and the kids rather than some distant hotel room.

At the same time, Carolyn continued to prosper. Her boss had decided to retire and Mr. Simmonds promoted Carolyn into the job of Division Chief. Her name was already a household word within the agency, but now she was one of the agency's senior managers. The word around the agency was simple: If you needed new positions in your organization, you had to get past Carolyn and her organization first. Her reputation said she was tough and smart, but fair and reasonable. Carolyn was the manpower guru in the agency. She was a grand lady, stood at the top of the management ladder, looked and acted the part better than anyone else. All of Mr. Simmonds' predictions had come true. Carolyn was now one of the executive managers of the agency, admired and respected by everyone. She had not one enemy in the entire agency.

Jim and Carolyn's life was so good, neither of them could believe their great fortune. Decoration of the new house was almost complete and just when they thought nothing could go wrong, the dark side of life suddenly showed itself, again. Jim's father died suddenly from heart failure. Jimmy had gone through heart bypass surgery very well and was recovering nicely. The Doctors had been optimistic for months, but in the end, nature had her way.

"Actually," his surgeon advised, "The operation was totally successful, but forty years of Camel cigarettes caused his respiratory system to fail. There was absolutely nothing we could do," the sad doctor reported.

Jim's mother buried him in the local cemetery beside other members of the family. The marker placed at his grave had both his and her name on it. Eloise missed her husband terribly, but she was a tough lady and soon adjusted to the lifestyle of a widow.

While the loss of Jimmy would seem to be enough, the dark side was not yet finished. It wasn't much later when Carolyn and Jim, after a tough week, turned in early to get some much-needed rest. About 1:00 am, the phone rang and the voice of Allen came across the line with a tone Jim had never heard before.

"Dad," Allen said, trying to calm himself, "There has been a horrible accident. I think Michael is dead."

Jim felt like something had hit him hard enough to take his breath away.

"Tell me what happened," Jim said sternly.

"Mike was driving ahead of me and he hit a patch of ice. Neither of us saw it until it was too late," Allen explained.

"Mike's car spun into the oncoming lane and a truck hit him broadside," Allen continued. "I hit the same patch of ice and spun in the other direction, going into a ditch. I am ok."

"What about Mike?" Jim asked.

"Ambulance arrived almost immediately. They are trying to revive Mike, but it really looks bad," Allen quietly replied.

"Which hospital?" Jim asked.

"Fairfax General," Allen replied.

"Okay," Jim replied. "See you there."

By now Carolyn had heard enough of the conversation to know Mike was in trouble.

"Is Mike okay?" Carolyn asked pleadingly.

"We don't know yet," Jim replied. "He is en route to the hospital. Get dressed quickly, we gotta go," Jim ordered.

When they arrived at the hospital, Mike was in surgery. The emergency room doctor explained that Mike had suffered a serious head injury and we would have to wait until surgery was finished before we would know much more. His heart had stopped, but the paramedics got it restarted at the scene. The injury was extremely serious. The night dragged on forever, but as the sun rose in the morning, the surgeon came out to talk to Carolyn.

"The damage to his brain was extensive," the doctor reported. "We have stopped the bleeding, repaired the damage as much as we can, and he appears to be stable. Now only time will tell. I wish I could be more positive, but frankly Mike is lucky to be alive at all."

The next three days were an endless nightmare of doctors and nurses tending to the unconscious child. Finally, the doctor met with Jim and Carolyn with the worst possible news.

"He will pass away any minute," the doctor announced. "There is nothing more we can do. His brain is shutting down due to the extensive damage. In turn, his vital organs are failing. I wish there was something we could do, but honestly we are helpless"

Within the hour, Mike was gone. Jim thought Carolyn would never stop crying.

"I always knew I would not want to live long enough to bury one of my children," Jim said, "And now, that horrible day has arrived. "I know I never want to see this again."

Carolyn and Jim buried Mike in the local cemetery and bought two other plots next to him.

"We will go here," Carolyn said. "With Mike. Someday we will be together again."

The loss of Mike created a sadness in Jim and Carolyn that would never in their lifetime end. It seemed like they expected him to walk through the door every day of their life.

"Learning to live with the loss of a child," Jim said to himself over and over, "May be one of the toughest lessons life can teach."

Slowly but surely however, life returned to normal. Jim and Carolyn concentrated on their jobs and the daily routine slowly returned. Robin and Allen had also been deeply disturbed by Mike's death but like everyone else, they soon learned how to live with it. Allen became disenchanted with school and told his father it was time for a break.

"I need to get away for a while," Allen explained. "I suppose you might say I am a bit burned out and need a new lifestyle at least for a short while."

"What do you have in mind?" Jim asked.

"I am going to join the navy," Allen announced.

"Sounds to me like you have given this a lot of thought," Jim offered.

"Yes, Dad, I have," Allen replied, sensing Jim was trying to understand.

"It does not mean I will not finish college. It just means that will come later. Right now, I really need this change," Allen said pleadingly.

Jim watched his son struggling with his choice of words so as not to disappoint his father.

"A very long time ago," Jim started, "Another young fellow I know had this identical conversation with his father. His dad understood and told him the military would not be so bad, but try communications/electronics school for a career field," Jim said, smiling at Allen.

Allen looked his father in the face with a sign of relief knowing his dad fully understood.

"And that would have been you and Granddad?" he asked.

"Yes, it was, and in the end, everything worked out well. I know you need to be your own master and figure out what course your life will take. I will only ask that you promise me to be careful, give the military your best effort, and try not to do anything really stupid," Jim smiled.

"You have that promise," Allen said. "And I will add, you will see me finish college in due time."

Jim hugged his son and within a few weeks, Allen was off to the Great Lakes Naval Training facility for basic training, then training at the navy's aviation electronics school.

The next six months passed quickly. The U.S portion of the network upgrade started on schedule. Jim and Roger Clark had completed the international agreement and both governments signed it without change. Bill Muncer retired and Rudy promoted Jim into the job as Operations Manager for the continental United States portion of the network.

"I am not going to replace you as Project Manager for the upgrade," Rudy counseled. "You have come too far and it would be too difficult to get a new manager on the ground before the upgrade is finished. If you find yourself a bit overwhelmed, let me know and I will get you some help but in the meantime, you are in the driver's seat."

"Thanks," Jim replied. "But there are two openings in the office for staff officers, I plan to bring some people I worked with while in my previous job. If I can get them, they will take up the slack and help me at the same time."

"Anyone I know?" Rudy asked.

"Yes, in fact I think you know both of them." Jim offered. "I will ask Bill Cormack to come in as well as Ron Green. Both are excellent telephone managers with just the experience we need here. They can help with the upgrade as task managers, then I will move them into permanent Account Managers when the new network is in place."

"So," Rudy said, "You plan to organize the military network much along the same lines as commercial telephone companies?"

"Sure," Jim responded. "While the managers are part of a military organization, the contractors that handle most of the day-to-day stuff are commercial. So, if we organize along lines they can understand, then the long-term functionality should be business as usual."

"I like it," Rudy said. "I look forward to seeing the final plan. I bet the General is going to like this," he replied as he walked away toward his office.

Doing double duty as a Project Manager and Operations Manager was demanding, but when the upgrade was completed, the function of Operations Manager seemed almost like a part-time job. Jim's reorganization fell right into place and the extremely talented staff handled everything efficiently and effectively.

The next two years were filled with the rewards brought on by the good life. Jim completed a number of major enhancements to the U.S portion of the network and established a national management organization allowing all the operating partners to share in development of policy and procedure for the network. Carolyn's successes also came one right after another. Very soon, agency General Officers consulted with her on almost every manpower related issue.

Robin married her college boyfriend Steve as their senior year came to an end. College graduation was followed by a small, family wedding. Robin and Steve set up housekeeping in an apartment not far from Jim and Carolyn's home on Prosperity Avenue and landed good jobs in their chosen career fields.

Within a year, Robin announced an addition to the family was on the way and if it is a boy, she promised to name him Michael. Jim liked the choice and began lobbying for a name in the event a girl came along. Jim and Carolyn liked Samantha, but Robin wanted to name a girl after her best friend Fallon. In the end, everyone agreed Fallon and Mike were great choices. Right on schedule, an eight-pound, six-ounce baby girl was born and, as promised by Robin, named Fallon Nichole.

The next three years passed quietly. Allen finished his tour in the navy and enrolled in Washington State University to finish his bachelors' program. When asked why Washington State, Allen replied, "There are two good reasons. First, after spending most of my navy tour at Whidby Island, Washington, it only seemed reasonable I would go there since I had been attending night school there for over two years. Secondly, however, the best reason is that they offered me a partial scholarship as a business major with a finance minor," Allen replied. "So, with the scholarship and the G.I. Bill, my undergraduate education is pretty much paid for - just like I planned." Allen was on his way to the top.

Robin's otherwise near-perfect life suddenly hit a major bump in the road. Steve and Robin mutually decided to call the marriage quits after two years. The announcement came as a shock to everyone, but Carolyn quickly recognized the problem this could present for Robin and her one and only grandchild.

"Move in with us until you can get on your feet again," Carolyn proposed to Robin. "We have a very big house with a lot of room and we can help you with Fallon," Carolyn offered.

"We can even help with a babysitter during the day while you are working if you wish," said Carolyn as she tried to make the offer irresistible.

Robin accepted and quickly moved back into the house with Jim and Carolyn. Fallon was soon enrolled in a daycare center that provided not only care for pre-school children, but also offered a pre-kindergarten education program. Fallon was entered into the program and soon became one of the best students in her class. Every day, Jim would play educational games with Fallon to help her understand the academic challenges she would face later in life.

The first game started with math.

"If Mommy gives you two pieces of candy and you eat one of them, how many do you have left?"

Little Fallon had been taught to add and subtract using her fingers and quickly learned to play the game successfully. Much to everyone's surprise, it would not be long before she would be solving algebraic equations off the top of her head. First grade math was going to be much too easy for her, but Jim saw a special talent in the little girl. She wanted to learn everything she could. Jim seized the opportunity to foster Fallon's education, disguised as a friendly little game. By the time she was five years old, her math and science skills were roughly equivalent to a child in junior high school, but Fallon's thirst for knowledge was far from quenched.

At a higher academic level, Allen was giving Fallon a run for her money. He finished his undergraduate degree with honors and immediately enrolled in graduate school at Washington State.

Jim was beyond delighted.

"I always hoped I would live long enough to see this day," he told Allen at graduation. "I can't begin to tell you how proud I am of you and all you have accomplished."

"Well," Allen replied with a sheepish grin. "It is either go to work or go back to school. Since the G.I. Bill is still in effect for me, might as well put it to good use. Besides, a business executive needs a master's degree sooner or later, might as well make it sooner."

Jim and Carolyn kept telling each other how well everything was working out for their family. Robin was going to night school working on her master's while holding down a lucrative accounting position with a large local company in the construction industry. Little Fallon was acting more like a high school student than one in grade school and the evenings together in the big house on Prosperity Avenue were happy beyond belief.

Unfortunately, Carolyn's mentor, Mr. Simmonds passed away unexpectedly. At the same time, a number of the older aunts and uncles on both sides of the family also passed away. The family that had been so large it was difficult to remember all the names was rapidly shrinking.

The years that followed were quiet and filled with all the joys family can bring. Finally, just after her fifty-first birthday, the agency announced an early retirement program. Carolyn learned she could retire four years early because she had already accrued over thirty-five years of continuous service. Because their savings and investment programs had gone so well, there was no reason not to. Carolyn submitted her papers and at the tender young age of fifty-one entered retirement!

While Jim was delighted, he was now faced with at least four more years of work before he was eligible. But the future was bright. Rudy had been promoted to an executive position in the agency, so he simply promoted Jim into his position as Chief of Worldwide Operations. Jim knew this was the pinnacle of his career. His new status as an executive within the agency would be the end of the line for his career. He was both proud of himself for all he had achieved, but humbled because he knew his successes had all been dependent on the faith his bosses had placed in him. Now his biggest goal was to make sure the world-wide network met all the goals of an ever-changing defense department and ready for the next test of ultimate performance – a war somewhere in the world involving U.S. military forces. Jim was determined to make sure the network would be more than ready for the job.

Chapter XII

Jim's first official act in his new job was to find a deputy. Rudy's deputy had retired and Rudy, knowing he was being promoted, decided to let his replacement, Jim, find a new assistant. Jim selected a young army Lt. Colonel who had just returned from a tour of duty in the Far East.

Steve Komack was smart, aggressive, and had a solid background in communications. He was not afraid to try something new or get his hands dirty.

"I suppose you will make Colonel and leave before we really get used to working together," Jim told Steve when making the announcement. "But in the meantime, you have all the tickets I need to get a few very important tasks completed."

"Not to worry," Steve later told Jim quietly, "My wife, Karen, and I have decided we want to stay in the Washington, D.C area, so I plan to retire when my tour here at the agency is complete and start my own business."

Steve's wife, Karen was a senior staff officer in the European Network Management Division and was also nearing retirement.

"And what about Karen's retirement plans?" Jim inquired.

"She isn't totally sure, but I think she will bail out in a few years. She wants to build a new home for our retirement, so once the planning is in place, she will probably hang it up," Steve said.

"Okay pal," Jim said. "Let's get our plan together and get the show on the road, we have much to do and not a lot of time to get it done."

From there, Jim brought in Mike Crandall to be his Interior Communications Manager. Mike and Jim had worked together when they were on active duty. Mike had retired from the U.S. Air Force as a Chief Master Sergeant, then hired on with the agency as a communications staff officer. Mike's wife Marilyn worked in the agency's accounting organization as a Senior Accountant. Mike's reputation as a Communications Manager was as good as it gets. During his short term in the agency he had already implemented a number of tough, complex policies allowing the agency to achieve early success in projects designed to upgrade and modernize the interior communications system supporting the entire agency staff. Mike was not afraid to tackle the tough issues and was more than thorough when examining all the details and alternatives. If Jim's group was to hold this overall responsibility, he wanted Mike at the management helm.

With the new team in place and their agenda agreed upon, Jim and Steve aggressively moved ahead. Success after success piled up and Jim was on top of the world. But then one morning as he walked toward his office after a lengthy staff meeting, he noticed an extreme shortness of breath. His heart was racing and he felt weak. Jim stopped, leaned against the wall for a minute until everything returned to normal.*This isn't right*, he thought to himself as he arrived at his office, sat down at his desk and told his secretary to hold all calls and visitors for a few minutes. Jim called his doctor and described the problem he had in the hallway.

"Is this the first time you encountered this problem?" Dr. Correy asked.

"No," Jim replied "but it certainly was the worst of the bunch."

"You have one of two choices," Dr. Correy ordered, "My office or the emergency room now!"

"I'm fine right now," Jim replied. "But since I am closer to you than the hospital, I'll be at your office in twenty minutes."

Jim called Carolyn and told her what happened. Together, they made it to Dr. Correy's office in record time. The following stress test, body scan, and heart catherization revealed a grim picture.

Three major arteries of the heart were better than ninety percent blocked.

"A major cardiac event is imminent," Dr. Correy proclaimed. "We need to get you into heart surgery like, yesterday!" he said.

"I have placed you on the schedule for Monday morning as an emergency. In the meantime, I will let you go home *ONLY* if you promise to do nothing more stressful than going to the bathroom! You need plenty of rest and be at the hospital early Monday morning. I will give you a strong sedative to help that entire process along and I will make all the surgical arrangements," Dr. Correy said firmly.

Dr. Correy tapped Jim on the shoulder with the finger of his right hand saying, "This is serious stuff. You could easily fall into a life-threatening situation. Follow my orders to the letter! Do you understand?" he said with a serious expression on his face.

Jim swallowed and replied with a weak grin, "I got the message Doc. I may be hardheaded, but I am not stupid."

Carolyn put her arm around Jim's shoulder and looked at Dr. Correy. "You can bet he will be a good boy," Carolyn said with a determined look. "I will see to it!"

Jim and Carolyn arrived at the hospital bright and early on Monday morning. Jim had the feeling the entire staff anticipated his arrival. With every step he took, someone new showed up at his side calling him by name and reassuring him that everything was going to be okay. Just before the anesthesiologist put him under, the face of Helen Alzer appeared into Jim's ever-narrowing field of vision. Helen was the mother of one of Robin's closest friends.

"Hi Jim," she said with a big smile. "It just so happens that I am the head nurse of the Cardiac Intensive Care Unit. We have been expecting you and I promise, you will get the best treatment available, I will personally see to that. okay?

Jim smiled. "I'm looking forward to it," he replied weakly.

Helen's face pulled away into the growing fog, then everything went black.

As Jim woke up, he could not see very well. Everything around him appeared to be surrounded in a pale gray fog. At that moment, the face of Helen Alzer came through the mist and they were nose-to-nose.

"Welcome back," she said with a big smile. "How do you feel?"

"Hmm," Jim replied, "Uh, no pain, vision seems to be a bit foggy, but improving, and everything seems to be working," he said as he wiggled his toes and tried to smile.

"You did really well," Helen replied. "Your doctor will be in shortly to give you all the good news, but you are going to be just fine. They installed three by-passes and now your heart is 100% normal," she said as she patted him on the head.

"You need anything right now?" she asked.

"Where is Carolyn?" Jim asked.

"She is on the other side of a window watching you. She has been there ever since you came out of surgery and has refused to move. She can see you right now and soon as your vision clears a bit more, you will be able to see her. Hold up your right arm and wave, gently," Helen ordered.

Jim did so and Helen leaned close to his face saying, "She is waving back with tears in her eyes. She knows you are okay now. We will get you two together in a few minutes. Ring the bell if you need anything," Helen said as she walked out of the room and joined Carolyn in the hallway.

Recovery went quickly and well. Physical therapy coupled with a big diet change had Jim back on his feet in no time. He could not believe how good he felt, all the time.

"If I had known I would feel this good, I would have had this tune-up long ago," he told Carolyn.

Six weeks later he was back at work and full of energy. Steve Komack had been acting in his absence and had masterfully moved their programs ahead with leaps and bounds. Over the next three years, everything fell into place nicely. Fallon was at the top of her class in every subject, Carolyn was doing some part-time consulting at a ridiculously high hourly salary and Allen had completed his master's degree. At his graduation, a large bank in Florida offered him a position in their apprentice program and he was off to Amelia Island to start a career in banking. Lori met and married Paul Foster. The two of them moved to New Hampshire where they started a business specializing in rescue and rehabilitation of abandoned or mistreated animals. While both understood they would not become rich, their work was a labor of love for both of them and the satisfaction was worth much more than gold.

As the three-year mark approached, the inevitable need for change became more apparent with every passing day. Steve and Mike decided it was time to retire. Almost on cue, doctors found a growth in Jim's bladder during a routine physical. Tests proved the growth to be a stage three malignancy and Jim was in real trouble. Jim knew this was not going to be an easy fight, so he chose to do battle in retirement. Jim, Steve, and Mike submitted their retirements and within three months, all three were unemployed!

Carolyn was shocked beyond belief at the bad news.

"Are you going to be okay?" she asked as if wanting Jim to reassure her everything would be okay in the end.

"Yes, Sugar bear," Jim replied, "It is going to take more than this to get your baby down," Jim promised.

The fight against cancer appeared to be one filled with all the disappointments normally expected with such a terrible disease. But Jim's doctor had other ideas. He convinced Jim to try a new treatment that had just recently been approved for use in the United States.

"The typical surgery, accompanied by radiation and chemo therapy has a fifty-fifty chance of getting you through this," Dr Hall announced. "But I have witnessed a tremendous success rate with this new treatment program and recommend you give it a try - we can always do the conventional stuff later if this doesn't work," he said with a reassuring smile. "It will be a difficult first year for you as you go through the treatment schedule, but with a little luck, you are home free after that," the doctor concluded.

Jim had witnessed the devastating effects of radiation and chemotherapy first-hand over the years as members of his family had struggled with the terrible effects of cancer. He did not want that for himself or for Carolyn.

"I'm willing to roll the dice," Jim told Dr. Hall. "Let's get on with it. I am now retired and have much I want to do in my life. I do not have time for cancer," Jim said firmly.

Dr. Hall had been right on target, the next twelve months of treatments were no fun at all. After the initial surgery and the following treatments, Carolyn was forced to assume the role of full-time nurse.

"I won't let anything happen to you while I am around," she told him over and over.

Finally, the year of treatments came to an end and life as Jim and Carolyn had thought it should be began to return.

"I will test you every six months, looking for signs of cancer," Dr Hall announced. "And if all goes well after five years, you graduate. We are going to see a lot of each other for a while but just between you and me, I think you have it whipped. Get on with your life and make sure you are not late for your appointments."

For the first time, Jim and Carolyn started planning their lives together in retirement. Until now, their only plans were day-to-day, going through the treatment plan, now, they had a lot of good reasons to start thinking about the long term. They joined forces with Steve Komack and Mike Crandall looking for a place to spend their 'golden years.' At the same time, Mike and Elva Lawton joined the group. Mike had been one of Carolyn's boss' during her years at the agency. The small group began their search for the right place to live in retirement.

Meanwhile, Allen met and married Joan. They both worked at the same bank and both were on the fast track to success. Joan had completed her master's degree in finance and was determined to be successful in her career. They bought a home in Florida and started planning a family. It did not take long for success to kick in. Both Allen and Joan quickly climbed to the positions of vice president and their first child, Abigail, arrived on schedule. Abby was a delight! Jim swore she looked just like her mother, but everyone else kept saying she was a carbon copy of her father. Both Jim and Carolyn loved the job of grandparents and played the role really well.

Finally, the search for a retirement home came to an end. The group visited a new, planned community just outside Williamsburg, Virginia called Stonehearst and fell in love. The community had a very challenging golf course, a country club, and sat out in the country far enough from Williamsburg to be away from the hustle-bustle of the big city. Each family bought a lot, built a new house, and moved in for the long term.

Jim and Carolyn bought a lot looking out over Lake Mill pond. The view was beautiful all year round. Both Jim and Carolyn had a good idea of what the floor plan of their new home should look like, but neither of them could quite find the right plans. They made sketch after sketch, but in the end, something was always missing.

One Sunday morning, Carolyn was going through a magazine while drinking her morning coffee. Suddenly, she squealed like a small child "This is it!"

Jim almost dropped his coffee cup at the force of Carolyn's enthusiasm.

"Look at this hon," she said, pressing a book into his hands.

There on the page in front of him was the layout they had been looking for, two floors and a full basement. There were two master suites, one on the ground floor and one upstairs. A finished room over the garage would serve as a very nice office for Carolyn and the basement could easily handle a large workshop for Jim. After making a few sizing adjustments here and there, they found a builder and held their breath until the preliminary drawings and cost quote came out.

"I thought this design would put us in the poor house," Jim told Carolyn after their meeting with the builder.

"Me too," Carolyn confided, "but it looks like we have more than enough to pay cash for the full ride."

"Yes," Jim confirmed. "With a little bit left over for Fallon's college fund," Jim concluded.

The contract was signed and construction began almost immediately. Carolyn and Jim visited the new home at least weekly to make sure there were no mistakes, but everything went as planned without serious incident. Jim had the landscaper plant a large number of Birch trees in the backyard so Carolyn could see them when she looked out of the large picture window at the lake. Carolyn loved Birch trees and Jim thought they would remind her of him every time she looked out the window.

Just a few months before Jim and Carolyn moved into their new home, Dr. Hall announced that Jim has successfully passed the five-year mark and could consider himself cured.

"Not nearly enough cancer victims can claim the success you now have," Dr. Hall said. "While there was plenty of potential for a bad outcome, that new treatment made this entire recovery process a relatively easy trip. Enjoy your life and I hope it will be a long one. I know you have heard it said we all must go sooner or later," Dr. Hall said thoughtfully. "But when your time comes, it will not be because of this cancer. This chapter in your life is over," he said at their last visit.

"I like the way you proclaim my total cure," Jim replied

"Thanks," Dr. Hall replied. "In my line of work, I do not often have the chance to do this. As I recall you are a science fiction fan, am I correct?"

"Yes," Jim responded with a big smile, "Star Trek is one of my all-time favorites."

"In that case," Dr. Hall said with a knowing grin, "Live long and prosper my friend."

Jim shook the hand of his savior and walked away thinking, *Okay, time to really get on with it!* Once again, Jim was on his feet and ready to start his life all over again. He felt like he had a new lease on life, the world by the tail, and had no intention of letting go any time soon! *Let me make sure I understand all this*, he thought while walking to the parking lot. *I retired because I was seriously sick, but never really thought for one second I would not recover. So, I have recovered and with no plans beyond that! Not really good. Carolyn and I need to get on with retirement and finish building that new house we have always talked about*, he concluded as he climbed into his car.

Building a new home, especially one you expected to live in the rest of your life, was a bit traumatic for Jim and Carolyn. There were so many options, so many choices to make, more than ample opportunity to make mistakes - ones you might later learn you can't live with. But in the end, everything turned out very well. The house at Prosperity Avenue had sold at a premium price so Jim and Carolyn had more than enough money to insure all the features they wanted were included in the new house. A small swimming pool, a hot tub on the deck, a workshop in the basement for Jim, and a private office for Carolyn on the second floor were all features making the new home a total labor of love for both of them.

On move-in day, Carolyn and Jim were determined to do enough unpacking to allow them to spend the night in their new home. The first piece of furniture to be assembled was the bed in the spacious master bedroom, then the unpacking of everything else started. Jim found the compact disk player, loaded a number of their favorite albums, then opened a bottle of German White wine he had been saving. Before long the unpacking stopped, the fireplace was burning brightly, dancing in the family room started, and the entire evening turned into a romantic event.

"It is only fitting that we initiate the new house on our first night," Jim told Carolyn as they danced together in the family room.

"Yes dear," Carolyn replied. "I see no good reason to wait until everything is unpacked and in place. Besides, once done, we still have about ten or twelve other rooms to worry about."

"In that case, my love, we should get started, there is much work to do here," Jim replied with a playful grin on his face.

Little unpacking was completed for the remainder of the evening, but the entire scene was painted in Carolyn's memory as one she would long remember and recall more often than she wanted.

The early months in Stonehearst were filled with decorating of the new homes for the Knight, Komack, Lawton, and Crandall families. Their new homes were located within a city block of each other, so almost daily 'Happy Hour' was convened at one of the homes where decorating plans were the first topic to be discussed in great detail. Exploration of the local area eventually started and the families soon found all the sources of entertainment necessary to occupy their every retired day. Steve owned a Harley-Davidson motorcycle and soon found a local veterans motorcycle club where his love for the bike could serve his other passion, helping military veterans. Mike and Jim volunteered their time to the local homeowners' association and quickly became committee chairs working to improve and sustain the new community for its residents. While time seemed to pass slowly, it seemed every day was filled with excitement and better than the one before it.

"This retirement stuff is without a doubt the best kept secret on the planet," Jim often said to his friends.

"If I had known it was going to be this much fun, I would have avoided the career and went straight into retirement," he joked.

That comment always sparked lengthy discussions and debates about years spent working for a living. But life can often be unkind. The dark side seemed to show-up when least expected. Jimmy Hecht died suddenly of a heart attack leaving Carolyn's sister, Peggy, a widow. Within the same year, both Carolyn's mother Geraldine and Jim's mother Eloise passed away. Both mothers had lived a long and happy life, but their passing was not easy for the family. Bob Patrick soon succumbed to a combination of cancer and diabetes. This left Jim as the family patriarch, but he knew his time could not be too far in the future.

Patsy Benning called to say that Trevor had been seriously injured in a construction accident. Trevor had accepted a position with one of the nation's largest commercial construction companies as a Project Manager. From the very beginning, he had been successful and quickly climbed the ladder of success to become the Director, Domestic Programs. Patsy indicated Trevor was inspecting storage facilities for heavy construction equipment at a job in California when the blade of a bulldozer fell across his right foot. The doctors had amputated his leg, just below the knee, but the bleeding had been serious. Because Trevor had developed diabetes about a year after his retirement, the outlook was grim, at best. Unfortunately, after a three-day fight for his life,

Trevor passed away. Patsy buried him in Arlington National Cemetery so he could be with his military friends he had missed so much after retirement.

After the excitement of moving into a new home, life settled into a normal routine. Jim and Steve soon went looking for and found a local firing range. During their military careers, both had qualified as expert marksmen and they often took their handguns to a local firing range to practice their shooting skills. Carolyn expressed a curiosity in handguns so Jim took her through a handgun familiarization course sponsored by the firing range so she could learn to handle a firearm. Carolyn took to firearms like a duck to water. She was a natural. From the very beginning, she was extremely accurate at any range.

"Tell you what," Jim told her at the end of the class, "If someone breaks into our home, I will simply give you the handgun and tell you to go get 'em. You would not miss. I certainly would not want you shooting at me," he said.

Before very long, Carolyn had her own collection of handguns and was always anxious to schedule a trip to the firing range for practice.

It was not much later when at about 2:00 in the morning, Jim sat up straight in the bed, looking around and listening intently.

"Bad dream, dear?" Carolyn remarked, wiping the sleep from her eyes.

"No," Jim replied, "Our alarm system makes a noise when a door or window in the house opens.

When the system is armed, all hell breaks loose if you open a door or window, but when it is unarmed, opening a door or window generates a three second alert tone. I know the system is not turned on, but I also know I just heard the alert tone."

"Are you sure, sweetie?" Carolyn replied. "I didn't hear a thing."

Jim opened the drawer to his night stand and pulled out his .357 Magnum revolver and flashlight.

"Get your gun, baby," Jim said firmly, "Someone besides you and me is in this house."

Carolyn did not hesitate. She opened the drawer on her nightstand and pulled out her Smith and Wesson .38 revolver.

Jim and Carolyn went from room to room on the ground floor, turning on lights and checking for an intruder. There was none. The basement was the last stop.

"Stay here at the top of the steps," Jim whispered, "I will run down the stairs and try to surprise anyone down there. Soon as I open the door, you turn on the light switch. Don't come down unless I get into trouble."

Jim quickly pulled the door open and in two large jumps was standing on the basement floor with his handgun extended in front of him. The basement light had been turned on by Carolyn and there, near the rear door were the two culprits!

Jim lowered his handgun and started laughing so hard, tears ran down his face.

"What's wrong, what's wrong?" Carolyn shouted.

"Honey, our home has been invaded by two terrible creatures," Jim replied. "Lower your firearm and come on down. Everything is okay."

Carolyn slowly ventured down the stairs one step at a time until she could see the full room.

The basement door opening to the outside was slightly open and just inside two small rabbits were huddled together, shaking with fear.

"I'm not sure who was more afraid, them or me," Jim said.

Now it was Carolyn's turn. She was laughing so hard she could not talk. The two rabbits were probably terrified at the sight unfolding in front of them. As Jim slowly approached the terrified animals, they quickly decided to retreat along the same route they came in and ran out the open basement door.

"I was working down here last night and was in and out through this door several times," Jim said.

"I suppose I neglected to fully close and lock the door when I was finished."

Jim and Carolyn checked every room in the house to ensure everything was locked tight, then went to bed - the excitement was over. As soon as their friends found out what happened, they nicknamed Jim and Carolyn as Rambo Jim and Rambo Jane. The joke would last long after all partners to the friendships were gone.

The following months and years were filled with golf, happy hour, and long trips to warmer climates when the weather at Stonehearst was too cold. Steve was suddenly killed in a motorcycle accident and Mike Crandall passed away in his sleep at the ripe old age of eighty-one. Mike Lawton soon followed after suffering a severe stroke.

Shortly after his eighty-fifth birthday, Jim and Carolyn were sitting in their family room watching a program on TV late one evening when Jim suddenly pushed back against the sofa and called out to Carolyn.

"Sugar Bear!" he exclaimed.

Carolyn could see the distressed look on his face. She moved over next to him and took his hand.

"What's wrong, sweetheart?" she asked.

Jim squeezed her hand tightly and gasped, "It hurts."

He pressed his free hand against his chest, laid his head against her shoulder, closed his eyes, and was gone.

As he had asked, Carolyn had Jim cremated and his ashes placed a silver urn. She kept the urn on the mantle over her fireplace so she could see it every day. During her remaining days in the house, she would talk to the urn as if Jim was standing there listening to every word.

"We are still together," she often said, "And when my time comes, Robin and Allen will place you in the casket with me so we can remain together as we were meant to be," she said.

Carolyn continued her quiet life over the years, enjoying the role of grandmother - even though the grandchildren were all now adults - and spending time with Karen, Marilyn, and Elva.

She remained in the home she had built with Jim because she always thought she could feel him near her. With Beverly Ramsey still in Virginia Beach, the two of them spend a lot of time together. Neither had lost their love for shopping and since both had relatives in northern Virginia, the trips there were almost always planned with both of them sharing the driving.

"Won't be long before we will need to buy motorized wheel chairs," Bev announced, "Then we can have drag-races on the beach. That should get a lot of attention real quick."

Every now and then the subject of Carolyn moving back to northern Virginia would come up, but she would end the discussion with a wave of her hand and a long dissertation on how much she loved her home by the lake.

"Besides, I know he is still here! Jim is still here. Sometimes, I feel like he is standing right here at my side," she often told anyone who would listen. "What assurances do I have that if I move, he can move with me?"

"I can't quite put my finger on it and I surely cannot explain it, but I just sense he is always near," she would say. "And besides, even if it is only the imagination of an old woman, I like the way it feels."

At this point, the conversation of her going anywhere was over. While such comments from a woman almost ninety years old would normally bring suggestions of senility or failing mental faculties, no one dared make the suggestion around Carolyn. Her mind was clear as a bell, with recall of details long lost to most. No one was ready to question Carolyn's grip on reality.

"I know, I know," she would say. "You think I am losing it. The old broad has finally gone off the deep end. But I would suggest you mind your words as well as your thoughts because one day all of us might discover that he has been here all along seeing and hearing everything that goes on. You know how Jim is, he would take you to task for any unkind remarks."

"Keep your eye on 'em, baby," she liked to say, shaking her finger in the air with a mischievous smile on her lips as if talking to her long-departed husband.

Since Jim's death, Carolyn had spent many happy hours engaged in a life-long passion – reading. In her favorite chair by the window, overlooking the lake, she had read many a good book. Almost every afternoon, she would sit in her favorite chair, reading love story after love story.

"Jim loved science and science fiction," Carolyn often explained. "He said love stories were like riding a roller-coaster with emotional ups and downs all over the place, but I'll stick with love stories. I think deep down inside, he liked a good love story just as much as I do."

Chapter XIII

"...the handsome Prince married the beautiful Princess and they lived happily ever-after."

Carolyn folded her hands on her lap and smiled, pleased she was able to come-up with yet another version of the ever-popular story.

"So, PaPaw, how did you like my little story about you and me?" she quietly asked as if Jim were sitting next to her.

Carolyn paused as if waiting for an answer, but as she expected, the room was silent. The only sounds to be heard were those of two small children breathing as they slept soundly. Carolyn slowly eased herself up and out of the chair and stared down lovingly at the two sleeping children. She tucked the covers up around the shoulders of each child and kissed each one softly on the cheek.

"Sleep tight my babies," she softly whispered as she walked to the door "You both now have the entire history of our family safely stored in your memories. I hope you will enjoy the story as much as I have enjoyed living it over the years."

She wiped a small tear from her eye and walked into the hallway. She checked the night lights on the upstairs landing outside the bedroom door to make sure the light was bright enough in case the children awakened in the middle of the night. After descending the stairs to the main level, she went through her nightly ritual of checking doors to make sure they were locked, turning off lights as she went, and finally, as she passed through the family room, affectionately patted the silver urn sitting on the mantle above the fireplace.

"Goodnight sweetheart," she said softly. "See you in the morning."

Everyone had gone to bed; the house was quiet, but in her mind, she could still hear the music being played across the lake outside her window. *Everyone is playing with the angels except me*, she thought as she finished her nightly check list.

Carolyn walked down the hall to her bedroom, taking one more look behind her to make sure she had not missed anything. Comfortable that everything was as it should be, she turned and walked into her bed room. Closing the door, she turned on the TV and went into the spacious bathroom to ready herself for bed. She began her nightly ritual by brushing her teeth.*Yep, they are all still there and all of them are mine*, she thought as she admired two even rows of shinning white teeth, each perched in its original place.

Soon the makeup was off, the comfortable flannel nightgown was on, and she was ready to play with the angels. *Perhaps I will run into my babies tonight*, she thought.

She pulled the covers back and settled into the almost too comfortable bed. *Jim would really like this bed*, she thought *This mattress is even more comfortable than the one we had together. That was a comfortable bed, but this one is unbelievable.*

After browsing through most of her favorite channels, Carolyn decided there was nothing worth watching on the TV. She turned it off, placed the remote unit on the bedside table, turned out the lamp, and pulled the covers up under her chin. It had been a long day and she was very tired. Perhaps now she could, at long last, warm up!

As she closed her eyes, she felt that tiny, familiar pain deep in her chest again. She pressed her long fingers against the skin.

"Yep, need to make sure Allen eats all that chili tomorrow so I won't be tempted. This heartburn is getting to be a real problem," she said aloud as if someone was there to hear.

She closed her eyes and drifted into a gentle world of sleep where her babies were playing with the angels.

She opened her eyes with a start! Something was not right. The room should be so dark you could not see your hand in front of your face, but it was not! She had the strange feeling she was not alone, her senses told her someone else was in the room!

Carolyn rubbed her eyes and sat up in the bed to look around.*Why do I feel so uneasy?* she thought.

She looked around the much too bright room. There standing next to the bed was Jim. She looked up at him and smiled in relief.

"Well," she said, "I suppose I should have known I would run into you soon as I went looking for an angel to play with. If I have to dream tonight, I suppose it should be about you again. It seems I have been thinking about you a lot lately, so I suppose it follows that I would be dreaming about you, as well. Now that I think about it, dear one, you seem to be in all my dreams lately. How do you do that? Perhaps that chili isn't so bad, after all," she said, growing short of breath after her lengthy speech.

Jim smiled as he looked down at her. "Truthfully, Sugar Bear, I have always preferred that your dreams be of me and not someone else. And yes, I really had to work at it to be in your dreams all the time. I just wanted you to know that I was close by."

"Dear," Carolyn said affectionately, "I have always felt that you were close by. The kids probably think I am losing it every time I tell them that but somehow, I can always feel you close to me. Did you hear me tell you good night a few minutes ago?"

"Yes, my love, I heard you. I have been with you all this time, my sweet," he responded.

"Remember the time you fell at the restaurant? I was there and tried to catch you, but it didn't work. I was so disappointed,that you hurt yourself."

"Yep, that was what you would call a real bummer," Carolyn replied. "I banged-up my hip real good."

"Yep, you sure did," Jim replied. "I had hoped the pain would go away but, as you well know, no luck there."

"It wasn't all that bad," Carolyn responded. "Just a little uncomfortable," Carolyn patted her bad hip as if to relieve an imaginary cramp. "

So, here you are in my dreams, what will we talk about this time, PaPa? Did you hear the bedtime story I delivered to Mike and Sam?" Carolyn asked with a knowing smile on her face.

"Yes, I was there," Jim replied. "And besides all that, I caught your little thought about me becoming a fairy tale," Jim chuckled.

The expression on Jim's face now became stern and very serious as he spoke in a carefully measured tone.

"To answer your question, I think it is time to tell you, this is not a dream!" A hint of excitement was clearly present in his voice.

"I can't wait to hear you explain this one," Carolyn said with a smile. "You were always a good storyteller, so I bet this one will be a whopper," she mused.

Jim grinned and held out his hand, "Yes my love, I think you are going to like this one better than any of the others. In fact, I think it fair to say, I have been waiting a long time to spring this one on you! "he quipped.

Jim moved closer to the bed with his arm outstretched. Carolyn placed her hand in his and felt the warmth of his skin on hers.

"First time today I have been warm," she said.

She swung her long legs over the side of the bed and felt Jim pull gently as she rose to her feet and stood beside him. As she came closer, she noticed he appeared much as he had in his youth. His thick blonde hair and clear green eyes warmed her heart as it had in the days of their youth.

"My, my," she said, "My dreams have made you look even better than I remembered. PaPaw, you have aged very gracefully, you do real well in my dreams."

"Thank you, dear," Jim replied "But this time, there is no dream, this is the real deal."

He placed his arm around her slender waist and gently turned her so she could see the bed.

There, laying on the bed, was Carolyn. Her eyes closed and her hands folded across her waist.

"It's not a dream, sweetheart," Jim said gently. "It's your time."

Carolyn placed her slender fingers to her lips in disbelief. The wrinkles that had been on the back of her hand for so long, were gone; her skin was smooth and warm to the touch. She leaned against her beloved husband for the longest time as the reality of what she witnessed came through.

"So," she exclaimed, "Does this mean I'm dead?"

"Yes, Sugar bear," he said thoughtfully. "That kinda sums it up," he grinned.

"Oh," Carolyn said with a shocked look on her face. "When our family finds me in the morning, this will not be a happy scene," Carolyn explained with a sad expression on her face.

"Only for a little while," Jim offered. "All of them, even Mike and Sam, have talked about this time and again and they are ready. Everyone has expected this for quite a while," Jim explained. "

"But, not to worry or be sad, we can visit them anytime we wish. They won't be able to see or hear us, but they will know we are close," Jim offered. "Just like last week when you stepped out of the shower. I was there and could not resist patting you on the fanny, but when I touched your skin, you jumped as if you felt it."

"Oh," Carolyn responded. "So that was you?" she asked. "Yes dear, I do remember. I would have sworn someone else was in the room with me, but I could not see or hear anything."

"Yep," Jim replied. "That has been going on for a long time. I never quite figured out how to get through to you, but I could always see and hear you clearly as I do now. I suppose by now you know those little chest pains you were having all day did not come from the chili," he continued with a questioning look on his face.

"Yes," Carolyn replied, "It all adds up now."

A broad grin spread across Jim's face, "If it makes it any easier for you, I prefer to think of this as getting started all over again. This has been like an intermission during our favorite play, I was anxious for the next act to begin. You and I have much to do together and plenty of time to do it," he said as he happily spoke of events yet to come.

A big smile filled her face as she realized they would never be apart again."So," she whispered as she became more comfortable with what she was seeing, "I'm here with you, we are together again, and we will be together for…?" she whispered softly as her voice trailed off from the silent question.

"Forever," Jim replied firmly to complete her question. "Forever Sugar Bear. There is no end to this play."

After a moment of deep thought, her face brightened, then a smile of understanding spread across her lips as her mind accepted the reality of the moment.

Jim held her face in his hands. "Remember that picture I carried of you when I was on my last tour in Germany?" he asked.

Carolyn blushed; she knew that picture was said by her friends to be the best she ever took because it made her look so young.

"I was only twenty-eight," she said as she recalled how Jim had kept that picture with him his entire life.

"If I took another one right now, no one would be able to tell the difference." He held his hands up as if holding a camera ready to take a grand picture of her.

"Okay," Carolyn said as she returned from her thoughts, "What happens now?" she asked.

Jim pulled her close, kissed her on the cheek tenderly, and whispered in her ear, "Oh, Sugar Bear, this is the part you are really gonna like... "

THE END... Really???????